TIME TRAVEL
TWINS

KU-760-991

THE
VIKING
ATTACK

JOSH LACEY
ILLUSTRATED BY GARRY PARSONS

ANDERSEN PRESS

First published in Great Britain in 2023 by
Andersen Press Limited
20 Vauxhall Bridge Road, London SW1V 2SA, UK
Vijverlaan 48, 3062 HL Rotterdam, Nederland
www.andersenpress.co.uk

2 4 6 8 10 9 7 5 3 1

British Library Cataloguing in Publication Data available.

ISBN 978 1 83913 333 6

Printed and bound in Great Britain by Clays Ltd, Elcograf S.p.A.

THE
VIKING
ATTACK

Look out for more in the
Time Travel Twins series!
Time Travel Twins:
Roman Invasion

I hate the Vikings.
I hate the Vikings.
I hate the Vikings.
They're so boring.

Scarlett read these words over her brother's shoulder and laughed.

'That's it?' she said.
'That's all you've written?'

'I've only just started,' Thomas said.

'You've been working on it for two hours! What have you

been doing all this time?'

'Thinking,' Thomas said.

Scarlett couldn't believe it. During those same two hours, she had written three more pages of her own history project. It was now eleven pages long, and she had illustrated it with a map which she had downloaded and printed out, plus six sketches that she had drawn herself. Her homework wasn't finished yet. She was intending to add another map, several more drawings, and at least five further pages of information about the Vikings.

'You'd better get a move on,' she advised her brother.

'I'll be fine,' Thomas replied. 'I've got ages.'

'No, you haven't. We have to hand them in the day after tomorrow.'

'Like I said, I've got ages.' Thomas stood up, yawned, stretched his arms, and wandered out of the room.

'Where are you going?' Scarlett called, but

Thomas didn't reply.

It was Saturday afternoon, and the twins were staying with their grandfather. Both of them should have been finishing their history projects this weekend, so they could deliver them to their teacher, Miss Wellington, first thing on Monday morning.

Miss Wellington had told them that there was going to be a prize for the best history project in their year. Scarlett was determined to win it.

She carried on with her project. Her brother didn't come back. Scarlett was so absorbed in her work that she didn't even wonder where Thomas might have gone or what he might be doing.

When she finished another page, she finally lifted her head and looked around, but she couldn't see him.

'Thomas?'

There was no answer. His project was still

on the table, exactly where he had left it. He hadn't written another word.

She called again, louder.

'Thomas? Where are you? Hello?'

Again there was no answer.

She went to search for her twin brother. She couldn't find him upstairs in the bedroom that they were sharing, or the bathroom, or anywhere else in the house, so she went outside to the yard, where she noticed that the door of their grandfather's workshop was wide open.

Scarlett went to investigate.

Grandad lived in a small house in a forest, more than a mile from the nearest neighbour.

He had chosen to live in this particular house for two reasons. Firstly, he liked privacy. And secondly, opposite the house was a large barn, which he had converted into his workshop. On the door was a handwritten sign which read

DANGER

DO NOT ENTER

Scarlett opened the door and looked inside. She saw Thomas standing with his mouth wide open, and Grandad peering at his teeth, and poking around with a little screwdriver and a pair of pliers.

'What's wrong with Thomas?' Scarlett asked. 'Has he got toothache?'

'No, his teeth are perfect,' Grandad said with a laugh. 'I'm fitting the translator.'

Thomas and Scarlett's grandfather had straggly hair which stuck out in every direction. Today he was wearing odd socks, and trousers with holes in the knees, and a jumper with holes in the elbows, and two pairs of glasses, one on the top of his head, the other hanging on a piece of string around his neck. If you met him, you would never have guessed that he was a brilliant scientist who had created several extraordinary devices which had the power to change the world.

Grandad didn't have a job. Instead he spent all his time thinking, dreaming, and working on his inventions. For the past few years, he had been building a time machine, an immensely complex and sophisticated piece of machinery which currently occupied most of the space in this big old barn.

No one could know what he was building here, Grandad always said. His work had to be completely secret. *If anyone asks what I do, say I work with computers. They won't ask any more questions.* And he was right, they never did.

Another of Grandad's brilliant inventions was a tiny machine which you fitted to your mouth, clipping it behind your front teeth, so you could speak any language. He had also invented a tiny earpiece which would allow you to understand anything that anyone said to you. Scarlett had seen both these inventions, but she couldn't understand why Thomas

should be wearing them right now.

'I'm sending him back to have a look at the Vikings,' Grandad explained. 'He needs some inspiration for his homework.'

Scarlett was shocked. 'You can't do that! It's much too dangerous. What if he never comes back?'

'He'll be fine,' Grandad said. 'He's a very sensible young man.'

'No, he isn't.'

'I am,' Thomas insisted.

Scarlett said, 'If you want him to travel through time, Grandad, why don't you go with him?'

'Someone has to stay here and operate the machine,' Grandad said.

'I could do that,' Scarlett said.

'You don't know how to,' Grandad said. 'But you can go with your brother if you want. You'll learn a lot about the Vikings too.'

'You must be joking,' Scarlett said to her

grandfather. Then she turned to her brother. 'Don't do this, Thomas. What if you get stuck in the past? Or murdered! What if the time machine sends you into the future by mistake? Or disintegrates you into a million pieces?'

Thomas nodded. 'You're right,' he said. 'It is very dangerous. Anyone sensible would stay here and read a good book instead.'

'Exactly,' Scarlett said.

'See you later,' Thomas said. He walked towards the doorway at the centre of the machine. 'OK, Grandad. I'm ready to go.'

Scarlett thought through her options. Could she really let her brother travel through time alone? Didn't she have a duty to look after him? If she couldn't stop him, shouldn't she go with him to make sure he didn't suffer some terrible accident?

She would have liked to sit down and consider the matter properly, maybe writing a list of pros and cons, thinking through all the alternatives, and discussing all the issues before reaching a conclusion and deciding on the most sensible course of action. Unfortunately, she didn't have time for any of that, because Grandad was already touching a screen on his time machine, spinning a dial, choosing the year where Thomas would end up. He moved the dial back a thousand years, then another thousand, but wasn't sure where to stop it. He looked at his grandchildren.

'When were the Vikings?' he asked.

Thomas shrugged his shoulders. 'I haven't a clue.'

'You don't even know that?' Scarlett couldn't believe it. 'We've been studying them all term!'

'It's not my fault if I'm not interested in history.'

Grandad was still waiting for an answer. 'Come on, kids. Tell me. When were the Vikings?'

Scarlett knew the answer. 'Roughly between

the year 800 and the year 1000, although you could say the Age of the Vikings started earlier than that and ended after that.'

Grandad touched the screen again, and moved the dial to 800, then nudged it forwards a few notches. For no particular reason, he settled on the year 859. Then he turned the machine's main switch from OFF to ON. A low hum filled the workshop. Lights flashed. Tubes gurgled. Cylinders shook.

Discs spun. Fluid pumped. The ground beneath their feet trembled as the enormous machine shuddered and whirred.

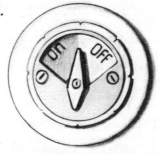

Thomas walked towards the door. It was open, but on the other side, there was nothing but darkness.

'Stop!' Scarlett yelled to her brother. 'You can't do this.'

'You can't tell me what to do,' Thomas replied. 'You're not my mum.'

'I am your big sister,' Scarlett said.

'You're not bigger than me.'

'I'm older than you.'

'Don't be silly.'

'It's a fact.'

Scarlett *was* older than her brother. And much more sensible. That was what she thought, anyway, and most people seemed to agree with her.

According to Thomas, they were the same age, but of course he was wrong. She had been born before him. Not very long, it was true. But twenty minutes was more than nothing, wasn't it? So she was the oldest, and he was the youngest, and so he ought to do whatever she said. Unfortunately, he never did.

Now he gave her a little wave.

'See you later,' Thomas said, and stepped

through the doorway.

'Wait,' Scarlett cried, but she was too late. He had already disappeared. One moment, he had been there, and the next he was gone. The darkness had swallowed him up.

Scarlett turned and looked at her grandfather.

'You really shouldn't have done that,' she said.

'Sorry,' Grandad replied with a cheerful grin. He clearly wasn't sorry at all, merely delighted that his machine had worked so well.

'Tell me one thing,' Scarlett said. 'How is Thomas going to get back again?'

'Oh, you don't have to worry about that. It's very simple.' Grandad held up a small device about the size of a phone. 'You see this button? He simply presses it once. That's all. Pressing the button activates the wormhole, which sucks him straight back again, and delivers him to this moment in time.'

Scarlett said, 'He presses that button right there?'

'Exactly.'

'While you're holding it?' Grandad stared at the object in his hand.

'Oh, dear,' he said. 'I must have forgotten to give it to him.'

'Grandad!'

Ten minutes later, Scarlett was ready. She was wearing two tiny translators of her own, one fixed to the back of her front teeth, the other tucked behind her right ear, so she could speak and understand any language. She had the device safely tucked in her pocket. She simply had to find Thomas, hold his hand, and press the button, then the two of them would be whisked back through the wormhole and delivered to their own time.

Scarlett felt nervous, but she knew she had no choice. She couldn't abandon Thomas in the year 859.

Grandad nodded to her. The machine was ready. As soon as she stepped through the doorway, the wormhole would link together two points in time and space, and deliver her from one to the other.

Scarlett would have liked some information about the time machine, the wormhole, and how they worked. Would she be safe? Had her grandfather used the time machine himself? If not, why not? And if she was trapped in the year 859, with or without Thomas, what was she meant to do next? Would they both have to spend the rest of their lives in the time of the Vikings?

She did try to ask some of these questions, but Grandad refused to answer them. He would tell her more about the time machine when she returned with Thomas, he promised.

'Good luck,' Grandad said.

'Thanks.'

Scarlett took a quick breath, then strode quickly to the doorway, and stepped into the darkness.

Thomas felt as if the floor was moving under him.

Rocking from side to side.

Backwards and forwards.

Throwing him around, knocking him off balance.

The wind whistled in his ears. The cold slapped his cheeks. He tasted salt on his lips.

He looked around. His grandfather's workshop had gone. Instead he saw the open sea, the vast empty sky, and a long wooden boat filled with twenty men, every one of them staring at him.

Twenty faces full of anger and confusion.

He could hardly believe it. Grandad's

machine actually worked. He had been sucked into a wormhole! Dragged through time and space. The whole thing had happened so quickly that he'd barely had time to witness what was going on. He had seen stars and the infinite blackness of space. He had been deafened by a noise like roaring thunder. His head hurt. His eyes ached. He felt sick. But where was he now? And who were these men?

As far as Thomas could see, they all had big muscles, broad shoulders, and fierce faces. Many had ponytails. Most had beards, some short, others long, and many of them decorated with beads and tassels. They were dressed in simple brown smocks. One man was standing at the back of the craft, both hands gripped around a long oar which he used to steer the boat. Down at the bottom of the craft, Thomas could see a jumble of food, clothes, blankets,

18

coiled ropes, barrels and baskets.

There was a moment of stillness, when all of them – those twenty men and Thomas himself – were too surprised to move. Or speak. Too surprised to do anything except stare.

Thomas knew he had made a terrible mistake. *Oh, Grandad,* he wanted to say. *What have you done? Where have you sent me?* He should never have stepped into the time machine without making some sensible preparations first – like bringing a weapon, for instance, and planning exactly where he was going to end up.

Luckily he could get home easily. He simply needed to press the button on the device that his grandfather had given him, and he would be whisked back to his own time.

Yes, he thought, he should do that right now. These Vikings looked vicious. He didn't want to be murdered by them. He reached into his pocket for the device, and fished it out, and

was about to press the button, sending him into the wormhole, when he realised that he was holding a fidget spinner.

It had been in his pocket all day.

What had happened to the device? Where had it gone? Had it disappeared in the wormhole?

Oh, no. Now he remembered. Grandad never gave it to him.

He was trapped here with no way to get back to his own time.

While Thomas was stuffing the fidget spinner back into his pocket, the twenty Vikings stared at him in silence. They must have been even more astonished than him, wondering how he had appeared here, suddenly stepping through the air, appearing out of nothing. The only noises were the wind in the sail and shrieking seagulls overhead. Then one of the men shouted out, 'He's a troll!'

'No, he's an elf,' cried another.

'Maybe he's a ghost,' suggested someone else. 'Or a shape shifter.'

'Whatever he is, we don't want him aboard,' said one of the other warriors. 'He'll bring us bad luck.'

'Let's kill him!' yelled a voice from the back of the boat.

This was greeted by a roar of agreement.

The twenty men reached for their weapons. A couple of them had swords. Others were armed with spears, axes, or knives.

Thomas looked around.

How could he escape?

Jump overboard?

Around the boat was the open sea. The shore

was only a narrow grey line on the horizon. He was a good swimmer, but he couldn't get that far.

This can't be happening, he told himself. *This isn't real. This is a dream.*

But he knew he wasn't asleep. The salt, the wind, the sea, and those armed men coming for him – this was more vivid than anything he had ever dreamed.

How was he supposed to save himself? What was he going to do? He didn't have much time to think about it, because these warriors were clearly men of action, more interested in fighting than sitting around chatting.

He didn't have any weapons. Unless you counted a fidget spinner, and he didn't. So how was he going to defend himself against twenty murderous men?

'Foul monster of the deep, prepare to die!' yelled a deep voice – which belonged to the man at the front of the crew, the biggest of them all, a huge bloke with massive muscles, a chain mail tunic stretched over his chest, and an axe clasped in his hands, its blade glistening in the sunshine.

'Wait, we don't have to fight,' Thomas said, raising his hands. 'It's always better to talk about things first, don't you agree?'

The warrior gave a contemptuous laugh. He wasn't going to fall for that trick, he seemed to be saying. He wouldn't believe the words that came out of the mouth of a mysterious creature – an elf, a troll, or whoever might be lurking inside the body of this boy.

Thomas watched in horror as the warrior gripped his axe with both hands and swung it into the air. Ready to come down on Thomas's head. And split his skull in half.

Scarlett was lying face down in a pile of poo.

And not just any poo.

Pig poo.

Which is pretty much the smelliest and most unpleasant poo that you can imagine.

The stench was disgusting. Scarlett wanted to throw up. But even worse than the smell was the sensation of sticky poo all over her skin and clothes, seeping between the gaps in her clothes, clumping her hair together, even getting in her eyes and nostrils and – oh, yuck! – her mouth. She spat, then rolled over, and wiped the back of her sleeve across her lips.

Someone was staring at her.

No, not some*one*. Some*thing*.

A great big sow. With little round eyes and a squat snout.

The pig let out an angry *oink*. She had a litter of piglets swarming around her, trying to get milk for themselves, and she clearly didn't like the fact that another creature had turned up, taking up valuable space.

Falling face first into a pile of pig poo is bad enough. Finding yourself face to face with an angry pig is even worse. But what made the whole situation absolutely unbearable for Scarlett was the sound of laughter.

'Ah-haha, haha! Ahhh-hahahaha!'

Someone was laughing at her!

Probably Thomas.

Who else would be rude enough to laugh at her like that?

Scarlett rolled over, sat up, wiping pig poo

out of her eyes, and looked around, searching for her twin brother.

To her surprise, the source of the laughter wasn't Thomas, although he did seem to be a boy of about her own age. A boy with brown hair, brown eyes, pale skin and cheeks which were turning bright red because he'd been laughing so much. He was holding his sides and rocking back and forth, so overcome by hilarity that he could barely breathe, let alone speak.

'Oh, yes,' Scarlett said in her most dismissive tone of voice. 'Poo is *so* funny, isn't it? If you're three years old.'

The boy stopped laughing. 'Are you trying to insult me?' he asked.

'I wouldn't bother,' Scarlett said. 'It's too easy.'

'You *are* trying to insult me!'

'I'll stop,' Scarlett said. 'If you say sorry for laughing at me.'

'What if I don't want to?'

'Then I might have to bury your head in a pile of pig poo.'

'Just you try,' the boy said.

'I will,' Scarlett said. She wasn't scared of him. She'd fought Thomas enough times, and beaten him enough times, to know how to fight a boy of her own age.

She stood up. The two of them faced off. They must have been about the same age. She was taller than him, but he had beefier muscles, and looked as if he spent all day doing vigorous exercise. His clothes looked old and shabby. He was wearing a simple brown smock which came down to his waist, a pair of dirty breeches and leather sandals. She thought he was probably the boy who looked after the pigs. Maybe the farmer's son. Had he seen her brother? She'd ask him in a moment, but first she had to fight him.

'Come on,' Scarlett said, putting up her fists. 'Let's do this.'

'I'm ready when you are,' the boy said.

They circled, each of them warily watching the other, waiting for the first sign of movement, an attack.

Down in the mud, the piglets squealed, and their mother made an impatient groan. She was suckling her eight little sons and daughters, all of them squabbling over her milk, and none of them took any notice of the boy or the girl as they paced around the sty.

The boy lunged. Scarlett jumped back, then shoved him away. He stumbled backwards, regained his balance, and threw himself at her. This time it was Scarlett's turn to dodge out of the way, but she wasn't quick enough. The boy landed a blow. Scarlett hit him back just as hard. Neither of them made a sound or gave any sign of being hurt. They circled again, both of them concentrating hard, ready to attack again or defend themselves.

Although they'd each managed to land a blow

on the other, the fight hadn't got serious yet, and never did, because they were interrupted by a shout.

'Alfred!' It was a woman's voice, raised in anger. 'Alfred! I can smell burning! Is that what I think it is?'

'Oh, no, the bread,' the boy muttered to himself.

Not giving a word of explanation to Scarlett, he turned, scrambled over the wattle fence, and ran across the grass.

Without even thinking, she darted after him.

⊣⊪∈ 4 ∋⊪⊢

Thomas stared at the shiny blade and knew he only had a second to save himself.

With one blow, that axe could cut his skull in half or chop through his neck, separating his head from his body.

But what could he say? What could he do?

Even if he had been armed, Thomas couldn't possibly have fought this warrior, three times his size, and armed with an enormous axe.

If only he had a phone, a torch, or even a box of matches. Something from his own time which would trick these men into thinking he was a powerful magician. People were always doing things like that in books and movies. Unfortunately, Thomas had nothing except a fidget spinner, and that wasn't enough to make anyone think he had magic powers.

He put his hands in the air, showing that he was unarmed, and spoke in a calm voice.

'You're making a terrible mistake,' he said. 'I am not a monster, I'm just an ordinary boy.'

'Then how did you appear out of thin air?' the warrior asked. 'A moment ago, we were sailing comfortably through the sea, minding our own business. And suddenly you're here, dressed in the strangest clothes I've ever seen. How do you do that if you're not some kind of monster? You must be an elf, a troll, or a magician. Come on, admit it, you're here to murder us with some terrible magic.'

The other men nodded and shouted their agreement. They urged the warrior onwards, suggesting he stop talking so much and start chopping this monster into pieces.

What could Thomas do? How was he going to convince them that he wasn't a threat? He could try telling the truth, but who would believe him? So he lied. He just hoped his story sounded a bit less crazy than the truth.

'I am Odin,' he said, looking the warrior straight in the eyes, and hoping his own expression gave no hint of the nervousness that he was feeling.

He remembered the name from one of their lessons about the Vikings. He never really concentrated at school. He had better things to do. Playing with his friends, for instance, or staring out of the window. But for some reason, he must have been listening when Miss Wellington told them about Odin, because he could remember a few facts about this particular Viking god.

Odin was a warrior. The owner of a horse with eight legs. He was the guy who had given his name to Wednesday. And he was married to a goddess named Frigg, who was the reason that Friday was called Friday. Thomas remembered that particularly, because he had put up his hand and asked Miss Wellington a question: 'If Wednesday and Friday are named after Odin and Frigg, why aren't they called Odinday and Friggday?' Miss Wellington had thanked him for asking such an interesting question, and explained that language evolves over time, and words change. Then she told the class a few more interesting facts about Odin, which unfortunately Thomas couldn't now remember.

Thomas would have expected the Vikings to bow down before Odin, or at least treat him with respect, but instead they greeted his words in a very different way: they all burst out laughing.

'Look at his arms!' one of the men shouted. 'He doesn't even have any muscles!'

Another yelled out, 'If he's Odin, I'm Thor!'

Now Thomas remembered another fact about Odin. He only had one eye. He had given the other in exchange for a drink at Mimir's well, whose waters provide you with infinite wisdom. These days, one of the other kids in the class had pointed out, he could have used Wikipedia, and kept both his eyes.

Maybe he needed to think again.

'You're right,' Thomas said. 'I'm not actually Odin, but I've been sent by him. He wants me to help you.'

'Oh, yeah?' one of the Vikings said. 'Help us with what?'

'If you put down your weapons, I'll tell you.'

'I've got a better idea,' said another warrior. 'We'll throw you in the sea. If you've really been sent by Odin, you can jump out again, and tell us how you're going to help us. But if you're a monster or a magician, you'll sink.'

That didn't seem very logical to Thomas. What if he was a monster who could swim? Or fly? Or what if his magical powers were so strong that he could simply zap them into nothingness with one click of his fingers? Then they'd feel pretty stupid, wouldn't they? But he didn't have a chance to point any of this out, because the warriors were laughing, shouting, and surging forwards, intending to pick him up and toss him into the raging waves.

But one of them had a different idea.

The enormous warrior with the axe was looking more thoughtful. He turned to the others. 'How do you know who Odin would send to help us? Have you ever talked to him? Have you asked him yourself?'

'I know he wouldn't send us a little boy with arms like twigs,' someone replied.

'He'd send us a bull, not a mouse!' said another.

'He could send anyone,' the warrior said.

He turned to look at Thomas again. 'If you've been sent by Odin, why are you here? Why did he send you?'

'Like I said, to help you,' Thomas said.

'Oh, yes? How are you going to help us?'

'I'll fight alongside you,' Thomas said. 'With my help, together we'll win any battle.'

Most of the men jeered or laughed, not believing him. They crowded towards Thomas, eager to throw him from their ship. They had been travelling together for a long time, and they were bored. They liked the idea of having some fun – and tossing a monster overboard definitely sounded like fun.

But one of them felt differently. The enormous warrior put himself between Thomas and the rest of the men. 'What if he *has* been sent by Odin?' He jerked his thumb at Thomas. 'We'd feel pretty stupid if we threw him overboard!'

'What if he hasn't?' one of the other men

asked. 'What if you're wrong, Olaf?'

'It's worth the risk,' Olaf said.

'I don't think so,' said another of the Vikings.

'Me neither,' said someone else.

Olaf pointed at Thomas. 'Look at his clothes!

Look at what he's wearing on his feet! Have you ever seen anything like that before? He must be a god of some sort. Why can't he have been sent by Odin?'

'Unless he's a troll or an elf,' someone else said to nods and murmurs of agreement. Why take the risk of allowing a monster aboard their precious boat? Why not toss him into the sea?

'It's risky to throw him overboard and risky to keep him,' Olaf said. 'So which risk do you want to take?'

'Throw him in the sea!' someone shouted.

Others joined in: 'Yeah! Go on! Feed him to the fishes! Let's see if monsters can swim!'

'I have an idea,' Olaf said. 'I'll vouch for him. If I'm wrong, and he's a monster, you can have whatever I earn on this voyage. You can keep my share and divide it between you.'

'If you're wrong, we'll all be dead,' one of the other warriors pointed out, but the rest of the Vikings didn't nod or agree this time. They thought Olaf might be right. Maybe this skinny boy really had been sent by Odin. And if he wasn't – well, then they could throw him in the sea, and each keep an equal share of Olaf's treasure.

They agreed to let Thomas stay.

'Come here,' Olaf said. 'You can sit beside me.'

He led Thomas along the boat. The other men stood aside to let them pass, peering curiously at the boy, still trying to decide if he might be an elf, a troll, or some other kind of monster, or just an ordinary boy.

There were benches down the middle of the boat, so the men could sit down and row with their oars, which were currently stowed away in the base of the longship alongside ropes, weapons, armour, barrels of fresh water, bags of food, and all the other provisions that they needed for their voyage. Big round shields hung from both sides of the longship. Up at the front, there was a carved dragon, its ferocious expression sure to provoke terror in anyone who saw the longship approaching.

Olaf and Thomas sat down together on a bench. The other men took their places.

Olaf asked, 'Why are you really here? What did Odin ask you to do?'

'I told you already,' Thomas said. 'He wants me to help you in your next battle. With me on your side, you'll win, whoever you're fighting against.'

Olaf looked as if he was pleased to hear this. 'Will we be rich?' he asked.

'Very,' Thomas replied.

Olaf looked even happier. 'What's your name?'

'Thomas.'

'Good to meet you, Thomas. I hope you're not really a monster, because if you are, I'll have to kill you.'

'I'm not a monster, I promise.'

One of the warriors returned to the stern, where he took the steering-oar with both hands, and altered course so the longship was heading towards the shore. That man's name was Bjorn Boatmaker, Olaf told Thomas, and he was the builder and owner of the boat. Another man stood nearby; he was the navigator, Olaf said, and his name was Erik Stargazer.

The sail filled with wind.

The longship quickly picked up speed.

They were heading for a gap in the hills, a river snaking into the interior of the country. They had decided to sail up that river, Olaf explained to Thomas, searching for settlements. A farm. A village. Or even better, a rich monastery, full of lovely treasure, gold candlesticks or silver ornaments, belonging to the monks, or their god.

'Nothing nicer than a monk,' Olaf said with an affectionate smile, perhaps remembering monks he had robbed in the past. 'They don't even fight, they just hand over their treasure. Turning the other cheek, they call it. Very kind of them.'

'Not far now, lads,' Bjorn Boatmaker called out from the back of the ship. 'We'll be there soon. Think of the treasure that awaits us! Think of the meal that we'll eat tonight! Fresh meat, my friends. I can taste it already!'

5

As Scarlett ran after Alfred, she got a chance to look at her surroundings. Had Grandad's time machine actually worked? Where was she? As

far as she could see, she had arrived in a little village on the bank of a wide river, surrounded by lush hills and thick woodland on either side. The landscape didn't look especially different from her own time. Trees, grass, sheep, goats, pigs – all of these existed in the present.

The village looked ancient rather than modern; it consisted of only a few houses, each built of mud and wood. The houses had

thatched roofs and windows without any glass, just a rectangular hole cut out of the wall.

Animals nuzzled at the grass in the surrounding fields. Three donkeys were tied to a wooden post. Chickens pecked the ground. A dog sprawled in the sunshine, fast asleep. Two teenage girls were sitting outside one of the huts, weaving rushes together to make a fence. One of the teenagers was pregnant, the other had a baby on her lap. They glanced curiously at Scarlett, and whispered to one another, then burst out laughing.

Yes, I know I look funny, Scarlett wanted to say. *I'm covered in pig poo! But you don't have to laugh at me! You could be a bit more friendly.*

She didn't say any of that. Instead, she turned her back on the teenagers, and hurried after Alfred.

She could see men and women busy with tasks, and children mucking around on the grass, playfighting with sticks. There was no sign of her brother. Surely the time machine would have brought him here too? Would he be hiding in one of the houses? Or sheltering in the trees?

What if the time machine had sent them both to the same year, but to different places? He might be a mile away. Or a hundred miles away. Or even on the opposite side of the planet. The landscape looked like England, but it could equally easily have been many other places on the planet; she had no way of knowing where she actually was.

She reached into her pocket, making sure that she had the device that she'd been given by her grandfather. It was still there. Waiting for her to press the button. One click and she'd be returned to her own time. If she had a problem, she would simply do that, then return a second time to search for Thomas. Would she be able to do that? Could she come back again and again until she found him? She wished she had quizzed her grandfather more about the exact workings of the wormhole and his time machine.

Don't worry, little brother, she said to herself. *I won't abandon you in the past.*

Scarlett always found her brother very annoying. Until he wasn't there, when she would, to her own surprise, start to miss him.

The boy led her to the largest house. Outside the main door was a smouldering fire. Five simple round loaves or buns had been put in a metal pan and placed in the embers to cook. Every one of them had been left too long, and had turned black, the dough scorched and sooty.

Kneeling by the fire was a middle-aged woman in a dark green smock. She was wearing two pieces of jewellery, a simple necklace of beads and dried seeds, and an ornate silver brooch pinned to her dress. She poked the burned loaves with a stick and shook her head.

'Will you look at this,' she said. 'Who's going to want to eat that? Didn't I tell you to watch the bread?'

'I'm sorry,' Alfred said. 'I got distracted.'

'I can see,' the woman said. She nodded at Scarlett. 'Who's this?'

'My friend,' Alfred said.

It was nice of him to say that, Scarlett thought. Particularly since he had done nothing except laugh at her, then fight her.

The woman gave Scarlett a hard stare.

'I've never seen this friend of yours before,' the woman said. 'Where's she from?'

'That's none of your business,' Alfred said.

'You're right, my lord,' the woman said. 'Of course you are. If she's your friend, it doesn't matter where she's from or what she's doing here.'

Scarlett looked from one of them to the other, confused by the relationship between them. Who was this woman? She couldn't be Alfred's mother or aunt, as Scarlett had initially assumed, because she'd just called him 'my lord' – so who could she be? His servant? If so, who was he? Was he really a lord?

The woman scooped the burned loaves from the fire. 'The pigs can have them,' she said. 'Unless you like the taste of soot?'

'I'm very sorry, Godwif,' Alfred said. 'I got distracted. I won't do it again, I promise.'

'I hope you won't,' Godwif said. Then her face softened. She turned to Scarlett. 'You'll want to clean yourself up,' she said. 'How about some clean clothes? Come inside, I'll find you

52

something to wear.'

Scarlett did as she was told, following the woman into the hut. Godwif handed her a cloth and some clean clothes: a tunic and a pair of leather sandals.

'Thank you so much,' Scarlett said.

She wanted to ask where she was – not just the name of this village, but the name of the country too – but she couldn't think of a way of asking the question that wouldn't make her sound weird.

Godwif left her to get changed. Scarlett wiped her face and hands with a cloth, then took off her dirty jeans and T-shirt, and put on the tunic. It had no pockets, but Godwif had provided a little cloth pouch, allowing Scarlett to carry around a few items. She placed the device inside, and fastened the pouch to her belt. Godwif had also given her a pair of leather sandals and some woollen ankle socks.

When she emerged from the hut wearing her new clothes, Scarlett looked around, and realised that everyone in the village – men and women, boys and girls – wore similar tunics. They had sandals like hers or simple shoes, sewn from a piece of cloth. Some people wore trousers under their tunics, others didn't bother.

Godwif held out her hands. 'Here, give me your dirty clothes. I'll wash them for you.'

'Don't worry,' Scarlett said. 'I'll wash them myself.' She didn't want to hand over her jeans, which would cause all sorts of complicated questions. Godwif would never have seen a zip before. Or seams sewn with a machine.

When Godwif hurried away to fetch the ingredients for more bread, Scarlett rolled her jeans and T-shirt into a tight bundle, nipped back into the hut, and hid them behind some shelves stacked with bowls and cups. She'd have to find a way to wash them later. She returned to her new friend, and asked him a question: 'Why did Godwif call you "my lord"?'

'Because of my brother,' Alfred said as if the answer was obvious.

'Who's your brother?'

'Athelbald.'

'Who's he?'

Alfred looked at her with a funny expression, as if he was unsure whether she was joking, or just a bit stupid. 'You don't know who my brother is? Really?'

'Really,' Scarlett admitted.

'My father, God rest his soul, was Athelwulf.'

Scarlett still didn't know who he was talking about.

'The king,' Alfred explained.

'Oh, King Athelwulf. Sorry, I didn't realise

you meant *that* Athelwulf.' Scarlett felt stupid. She'd read so much about the Vikings recently, but she'd forgotten about the people who had fought against them, the rulers of the countries in what was now the United Kingdom. Had she heard of Athelwulf before? She didn't recognise the name. But Alfred . . . yes, of course, she knew that name. She remembered reading about King Alfred. Could this be him? Or a relative of his? An ancestor or a descendent? She couldn't remember when King Alfred had lived. Would he have been alive in the year 859?

'If you're the son of Athelwulf, why are you living here in this village?'

'I'm here because I've been ill recently. I've spent most of the winter confined to my bed. My brother, the king, has sent me here to get some sea air. Godwif was my wet nurse, and she's looking after me now. I've been feeling stronger every day. Soon I'll be fit enough to go

56

back to the palace.'

Scarlett was still puzzled. 'You're the king's brother. You might be the king one day. Is it really safe for you to be staying here? Do you have any guards?'

'One,' Alfred said.

'What if someone attacked you? Or tried to kidnap you? Shouldn't you be living in the palace?'

'No one knows I'm here,' Alfred said. 'Anyway, I'll never be king. My father had five sons, and I'm the youngest of them all. The smallest, the skinniest, and the sickest. No one would ever want me to rule over them. I don't mind. I wouldn't want to be king. My brothers love nothing more than fighting and hunting, but I'm not a warrior. I prefer thinking. And dreaming. And reading books.'

'You're like me,' Scarlett said. 'I love books too.'

Alfred was very surprised. 'You can read?'

'Yes.'

'How did you learn?'

She didn't want to tell the truth. How could she say that she'd studied at school? In the year 859, there probably weren't any schools. A little village certainly wouldn't have one. Instead she pretended that she had been taught to read by a priest.

'I didn't know they would teach a girl,' Alfred said.

'They made an exception for me.'

'That's amazing. Maybe one day they'll teach you to write too.'

'You never know,' Scarlett said.

6

As the longship ploughed through the water towards the coast, Thomas quizzed Olaf about himself and his fellow Vikings. Olaf was happy to talk. He'd been aboard this longship for three weeks now, sailing first across the sea from their home to the coast of England, then making their way around the coast, looking for villages to attack. So far they hadn't had much luck, Olaf said. They had been battered by a storm. They had raided a few farms and villages, but had either been driven away by heavily armed locals, or picked on settlements so poor that they didn't have anything worth stealing. Now they were planning to land again, hoping to find a rich village with no guards, and steal some food and treasure.

Thomas assumed that Bjorn Boatmaker was the captain of the longship, and the leader of all the men aboard, but Olaf told him that they didn't have anything like that.

'We don't like captains,' Olaf said. 'We don't like kings either. Or earls. We are free men! We don't like being told what to do – by anyone.'

'Me neither,' Thomas said.

He was puzzled by one thing. He remembered Miss Wellington telling the class that the Vikings had kings with armies. Why didn't Olaf and his friends have a king? How had he avoided being told what to do by anyone?

'They have tried,' Olaf said. 'But we tell them to get lost. They come to our village every few years. Some self-important king who loves nothing more than ordering other people around. Some rich man who thinks his money allows him to do whatever he wants. They always want us to join their battles. To fight for them. To get killed for them. They make all sorts of promises, like "We'll give you more money than you can imagine, you'll never need to work again!" But we don't believe them. We've heard enough lies from kings and lords. We prefer to look after ourselves.'

Bjorn Boatmaker owned the longship, but he didn't decide where they went or who they attacked. Together, he, Olaf and the other warriors voted on which direction to go and what to do when they arrived at their destination. They worked together, made decisions together, and shared their winnings. When they sacked a village, a farm, or a monastery, they would add together all the treasure that they had looted, then divide it between anyone who survived the battle. Everyone got an equal share, except Bjorn Boatmaker, who received an extra portion to pay him for the use of the longship.

Many of the Vikings were wearing one or

two silver arm rings. Olaf explained that this was how they carried their wealth, rather than using money.

At the end of the summer, by the time they had finished all their raids, each of these Northmen hoped to be wearing a whole string of silver rings, stretching from their wrists to their shoulders.

According to Olaf, the men aboard knew one another well. They had grown up in the same village, or one of the farms nearby. Several of them were actually related. Olaf pointed out three of his cousins, and several neighbours who he had known for his entire life.

'Did you go to school with them?' Thomas had asked.

'Go to *what?*' Olaf didn't understand that word.

'School,' Thomas said. 'The place you go when you're a kid. To learn things.'

'Like what?'

'To read and write.'

Olaf still looked confused. 'My only teacher was my father. He taught me how to farm and how to fight. Is that what you mean?'

'Sort of,' Thomas said. 'Where is your dad now? Did he stay at home this year?'

'No, he has gone to Valhalla. He went a-viking ten years ago, but he never came back.'

Thomas was the youngest person aboard the longship, although there were a few teenagers, only a few years older than him.

The youngest was a boy who couldn't have been much older than Thomas, a teenager, only thirteen or fourteen years old, with a few wisps of hair on his chin. His name was Harald Littlebeard.

'Maybe he'll get a new name when he's older,' Olaf said. 'Or maybe he won't, we'll have to wait and see.'

Thomas wanted to know more about Olaf's life. When did he first go on a voyage like this one?

'In my fourteenth summer,' Olaf replied proudly. 'I was a big lad, so the fighting men took me with them. The smaller boys stayed at home, working in the fields. Only the toughest and bravest of us choose to go a-viking. Some men spend their entire lives in their villages, never seeing anything but their own fields and hills. I wouldn't want to be like that. Maybe I'll go home rich, or maybe I'll die on a foreign beach. Only the gods know what is coming.'

7

Godwif returned with the ingredients for making more bread. She brought a jug of water and a pot full of roughly-ground flour. Alfred might have been the king's son, but Godwif didn't treat him like anyone special; she ordered him to fetch a large bowl, and told him to get a move on, they didn't want to spend all day making bread, especially since he'd already ruined the first batch.

Scarlett had seen her father making bread at home, but his technique was very different to Godwif's. Dad had often encouraged his children to help, so Scarlett knew exactly what to do. You mixed flour, water and yeast in a bowl, kneaded the dough in a big saggy wet ball, which you left to rise for a few hours. Then you kneaded it again, shaped it into a loaf, and left it alone for another hour. Finally you turned up the oven as hot as it would go, then baked the loaf for forty minutes.

The houses in this little village didn't have ovens, just an open fire, so Godwif made a different type of bread, more like modern flatbread or pitta bread.

 She poured some flour into the wooden bowl, added some water and a little salt, then asked Alfred and Scarlett to mix the dough. They took turns to mix the sticky mixture, then shaped it into small round balls, each about the size of a fist.

Godwif and Alfred asked a few questions about Scarlett's home, her family and her village, which she answered vaguely, not wanting to give away anything about herself.

As soon as she could, she changed the subject, asking if they had seen a boy recently.

'I'm looking for my brother,' she explained. 'He's the same age as me. Have you seen him?'

Alfred shook his head. 'There are always strangers passing through, but I haven't seen a boy around here. Not recently, anyway. I can ask around. What's his name?'

'Thomas.'

'A good Bible name,' Godwif said.

Scarlett felt worried. What could have happened to Thomas? Why hadn't the time machine brought him here to this village? What would she do if he had been sent to a different place or a different time? How could she find him?

Godwif added a few small sticks to the fire, and stirred the embers. Scarlett and Alfred placed their dough in the pan, which they put on the fire to bake. There was room for only four pieces of bread in the pan, leaving another four to cook once these were finished.

Godwif said, 'This time, you won't let them burn, will you?'

'Of course not,' Alfred said.

'I'll keep an eye on him,' Scarlett said. 'Make sure he behaves himself.'

'I'm glad to hear that,' Godwif said. 'I wouldn't want to waste another batch of dough.'

She hurried away to check on her daughter, the teenager with the baby, leaving Alfred and Scarlett to watch the bread.

'Pull!' Bjorn Boatmaker shouted to the crew, setting a rhythm for their rowing. 'Come on, lads. Think of the treasure that we're going to loot today. Think of the feast we're going to eat tonight. Pull!'

The longship surged through the water, heading up the river.

They had used the sail to power their longship until they came closer to the shore. Now they were heading up the river, where the wind was less reliable, the breeze swooping over the hills, changing speed and direction all the time, so the twenty men aboard had lowered their oars into the water.

Pulling an oar was extremely hard work.

Especially if you were a kid who had never done it before today. Thomas's arms had already begun to ache, and he could feel drops of sweat on his forehead and in his armpits. Luckily for him, he was sharing an oar with Olaf, who was as strong as two ordinary men, and did most of the work.

Thomas took his hands from the oar, reached under his cloak, and checked his weapons. A knife was fastened to his belt. Slung over his back, he carried a small axe. When they reached land, he would grab one of the shields hanging over the side of the boat; Olaf had already pointed out the spare one that he could use. Olaf had also lent him a leather tunic, which would protect him in a battle, he promised, although it was much too big for Thomas, and reached down beyond his knees.

Although some of the Vikings still seemed to be annoyed that they hadn't been allowed to throw the monster overboard, others liked

70

the idea that Odin had sent a special warrior to fight alongside them, bringing them luck in the battle ahead.

Thomas hoped no one could tell how he was feeling. The truth was he was terrified of the battle ahead. He'd never really fought anyone. Scrapping with Scarlett or other kids in the playground wasn't much preparation for fighting alongside a bunch of bearded Vikings armed with spears and axes. He hoped they'd find a monastery. That would be perfect. Some friendly monks who handed over their treasure with a smile.

'Pull your oars, lads!' Bjorn Boatmaker yelled again. 'Pull! Pull! Not much further now. Pull!'

Alfred flipped the bread over halfway through the cooking process, so it browned on both sides, and the four little loaves were done by the time Godwif bustled back, bringing two cups of milk fresh from the cow and still warm.

Godwif reached into one of the pouches hanging from her belt, pulled out a piece of cheese wrapped in cloth, and broke off two pieces.

'Here you go,' she said, handing a cup and some cheese to each of the children.

The bread was warm and crispy, and tasted delicious, and Scarlett gulped down two loaves while Godwif was cooking the second batch.

Alfred wiped his hands on his trousers. He said, 'Do you want to see a book?'

'Sure,' Scarlett said.

'I own two,' Alfred said proudly.

Two books? What was so amazing about owning *two* books? If Alfred had owned a library, the shelves crammed with thousands of books, then Scarlett might have understood why he thought he was so special. But who was going to be impressed by someone who owned two books?

Oh, yes, she was in the year 859. The printing press wouldn't even be invented for several centuries. Each book had to be copied out by hand, word by word, sentence by sentence, page by page.

Scarlett didn't want to tell Alfred about printing, let alone ebooks or the internet, because he'd immediately think she was crazy. She had to carry on pretending that she had always lived in this time.

They went into the hut.

Alfred went over to a wooden chest, opened the lid, and carefully removed two books, each wrapped in a cloth.

They sat on the ground. Alfred unwrapped the first book, and gave it to Scarlett. She handled it carefully, appreciating that the book had great value to him.

Each book had a thick cover, made of leather, which looked more like carved wood than the paper cover of a modern book. The pages were also much thicker than the pages of modern books, and each of these books was surprisingly heavy. Scarlett carefully turned the pages. She pored over the text. She could recognise a few letters here and there, but couldn't understand the words. They were written by hand, not printed, and the letters were ornate, complex, and impossible to read. Scarlett couldn't even tell what language they were in. English? Latin? Or something else? Unfortunately her translator didn't work for writing, only speech. When she got home, she would have a suggestion for Grandad's next invention . . .

First Alfred showed her a book of poetry that he had won in a contest when he was a little younger. His mother had shown the book to him and his brothers, and promised it to whichever of them could learn one of its poems first.

'I couldn't actually read then,' Alfred recalled. 'So I persuaded our priest to recite the poem to me over and over again, and I learned it off by heart. So my mother gave the book to me.'

Next Alfred handed her a second, smaller book, which was a copy of St Matthew's gospel. Scarlett traced the letters with her finger, and looked at the beautiful illustrations dotted among the text. Animals, plants and people curled around the letters. Turning the pages, Scarlett found a capital S in the shape of a snake, a T which looked like a tree, and an R which bloomed with petals and leaves.

It was amazing to think that someone, or several people, had copied out this entire book. Tracing every word. Drawing every picture. Spending weeks, even months, and perhaps years, to create a single book.

'I got this when my father died,' Alfred told

her. 'My brothers could have had it, but they weren't interested. They quarrelled over his swords and helmets, but they left the book to me.'

'It's lovely,' Scarlett said.

Alfred said, 'If I ever became king of Wessex, I would teach everyone to read.'

'Why don't you suggest it to your brother?'

'He doesn't care about books. He can't even read. He doesn't understand that books are the most important thing in the world. They're what make us different from animals.'

'What do you mean?' Scarlett asked.

'Animals are mostly the same as us, aren't they?' Alfred said. 'They eat, they sleep. They live, they die. They even talk to one another in their own ways. But we're different, because we can talk to the dead – through the words in a book. I can hear the thoughts and ideas of a man who lived in a different city, a different country, a different time – through his words in a book. I never met my grandfather, but I can read the words that he wrote in a letter. I might be killed in a battle before I have a chance to meet my own grandchildren, but I could write a letter for them, or a book, and they could hear my voice. They could discover what I think. If I was king, I would make sure that every boy in Wessex could read and write.'

'And every girl?' Scarlett suggested.

Alfred thought about this for a moment, then nodded. 'Yes, why not? Girls should learn to read and write too, you're right. Everyone should. So we can pass our knowledge to our children, and our children's children.'

10

Across the placid water, on the nearest bank, barely ten metres away, Thomas saw a young man sitting on the grass.

No, not a man – a boy, a teenager, not much older than Thomas himself.

Maybe he was a shepherd, because he was surrounded by sheep and lambs, grazing on the riverbank's lush grass.

But he was also a dreamer, because he was clearly lost in thought. He didn't notice the longship until it had drawn level with him. At that moment, he must have heard the splash of the oars, or caught a glimpse of movement from the corner of his eye, because he slowly turned his head – and stared in amazement at

the longship with its carved dragon prow and crew of twenty fierce warriors.

For a moment, the shepherd boy was too shocked to move. His mouth dropped open. He stared at them in horror and astonishment.

Then he leaped to his feet, turned around, and started sprinting towards the shelter of the forest. Without giving his sheep a backward glance. All his duties forgotten.

The sheep didn't care. They carried on

nibbling the lush grass.

One of the Vikings yelled at the others, 'Stop! Stop! Stop the boat!' Once they had all lifted their oars from the water, letting the longship drift onwards, borne against the current by momentum, he leaped to his feet and addressed his comrades. 'Let's go after that shepherd and kill him! He might be carrying a bag of silver! Or a decent knife. Quick! Get the boat to shore! Don't let him get away!'

Another Viking also wanted to beach the boat, but he wasn't interested in chasing the shepherd. Instead, he wanted to slaughter some of those sheep.

'Roast lamb,' he said. 'Mmmm, I can taste it already.' He licked his lips. 'Come on, guys, let's stop working so hard, and treat ourselves to a decent meal.'

Olaf disagreed with both of them. 'I haven't come this far just to steal some sheep! I could do that at home. Let's carry on and get a decent haul. Something to make the journey worthwhile.'

'I'll fight better if I've had a good meal,' another of the men argued.

'You always fall asleep when you've eaten.'

'Are you calling me lazy?'

The argument went on for a while, some of the Vikings wanting to stop and gorge themselves on fresh meat, others determined to continue till they found a better target. Everyone seemed to have a different opinion, and they all wanted to be heard.

Eventually, the twenty Vikings had a vote. Without a leader, the best way to make a decision was either fighting or voting, and none of them wanted to waste energy fighting one another when they were about to meet a real enemy.

'Who votes to stay here and eat?' Bjorn Boatmaker asked.

Ten hands went up.

'Who votes to keep going?' Bjorn said.

He put his own hand up, and nine of the crew joined him.

It was a dead heat. What were they going to do?

Bjorn turned to Thomas.

'You can have the deciding vote,' he said.

'Me? Why?'

'You've been sent by Odin, haven't you? You must know what you're doing. What would be best? Should we feast on fresh sheep or keep sailing down this river till we find a better treasure?'

Thomas wasn't hungry. 'Let's keep sailing,' he said.

Bjorn ordered the men back to their positions. Some grumbled, others were pleased to be sailing further, but none of them made a fuss. They all accepted the vote. They agreed it was a fair way to reach a decision.

Olaf patted Thomas on the back. 'Good choice,' he said. 'You're a man after my own heart. Feasting can wait. Fighting comes first.'

Thomas felt pleased with himself, and glad that he had made a new friend in Olaf.

'Onwards!' Bjorn called out to them from the stern of the boat. 'Pull, lads! Pull with all your strength!'

Soon they picked up speed. The longship cut through the water like a knife, leaving a frothy trail on the river. No one spoke. Their minds were concentrated on the battle ahead. They had travelled across the sea, all the way from their own village, braving the wind and the waves, enduring cold and hunger, and now they were ready to fight. To kill. To steal. And to go home rich men, laden with treasure. What might they find? Gold? Silver? Swords and shields? Or just the ingredients for a massive feast? They couldn't wait to find out. All of them pulled on their oars, thinking about the battle that they would be fighting very soon.

The river curled around a big bend, then another, and Thomas got his first sight of the village. He saw sheep and goats in the pasture. He could hear a yapping dog, its bark carrying clearly across the water. Smoke curled gently from several of the little houses, which had thatched roofs and wooden walls. Inside each of those cosy little huts, Thomas imagined, the inhabitants might be cooking a tasty stew for themselves. Chatting and laughing. Making plans. Discussing what to do with the rest of this beautiful sunny day.

It was a peaceful scene. No one had yet noticed a longship on the river, heading towards them.

Thomas felt sorry for the inhabitants of that village.

They didn't know what was coming.

11

Scarlett heard a strange noise. Distant. Not loud. But quite clear. She lifted her head, held her breath and listened again, trying to work out what the noise had been.

Some kind of whistle, maybe.

Not the cheerful, carefree whistle of a person who was walking through the fields, enjoying the sunshine, planning what to cook for tea.

No, this had been a desperate whistle. As if someone had lost their dog, for instance, and was rushing up and down, calling out to her, begging her to come home again.

'What was that noise?' she said.

Alfred lifted his head from his book. 'Which noise?'

'Listen.'

They were sitting on the ground, each of them looking at a different book. Alfred had the gospel, while Scarlett looked at the pictures that accompanied the poems. Now they both stopped reading, and listened, waiting for the noise to be repeated. Just as Scarlett was beginning to wonder if she'd imagined it, she heard the same shrill whistle a second time, a little louder than before.

'The alarm,' Alfred cried. He jumped to his feet. Moving quickly but carefully, he wrapped up both books, and returned them to their home in the wooden chest. Then he hurried out of the hut.

'What's going on?' Scarlett asked.

Alfred didn't hear her, he had already gone. She darted after him.

An old man was hobbling down the hillside towards the village. He stopped whistling once he saw that he had alerted the villagers, and put his head down and ran as fast he could. Unfortunately that wasn't very fast at all, which was why Alfred and Scarlett sprinted in his direction. By the time that they reached him, the man was panting so hard that he could hardly speak, but he managed to blurt out a few words.

'They're coming!' he said. 'Bradwin sent the signal.'

'How many are there?' Alfred asked.

The old man didn't know. He had heard the signal, nothing more, so he couldn't give any more information about the invasion.

'What's going on?' Scarlett asked again.

Alfred paused for a moment to explain. He had instructed the local shepherds and farmers to warn him if they saw any intruders or invaders approaching the village, either over the hill or from the sea. They had set up a system of signals, passing a warning from one to the next, so he could be alerted about an attack.

He started issuing orders, telling the villagers to gather their belongings.

'You know what to do,' he said. 'Take as little as possible. No more than you can carry easily. And be quick! They'll be here very soon. Go! Go!'

A few villagers had questions for Alfred, but before they could even put them into words, a shout went up. Someone pointed down the river. Everyone turned to look. There, coming around the corner, was a longship.

For a moment, no one moved or spoke. The villagers all gazed at the boat, gauging its size, and trying to count the number of men aboard. They could only see one ship, but there might be more following behind. Ten, twenty, or even a hundred longships, bringing an army to ravage the Kingdom of Wessex.

Alfred clapped his hands, and shouted at the villagers. 'Come on! Move! Get going!

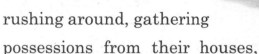

We have to get away before they arrive!'

As if they had been woken from a dream, the villagers started rushing around, gathering possessions from their houses, loading themselves with whatever they could carry. They didn't want to slow themselves down by taking too much, but they knew that the Vikings would steal or destroy whatever they left behind.

Scarlett stared at the longship and remembered her homework, her history project. She had spent days poring over pictures of Viking invaders, their wild eyes and crazy expressions, their swords and axes, their ferocity and determination, their eagerness to kill and steal. And here they were, sailing up this river, coming for her. She reached into the pouch attached to her tunic and fingered

the device. If she pressed the button now, she would be returned to the safety of her own time. Her absence wouldn't even be noticed. Alfred and the villagers would be too busy defending themselves, they wouldn't worry about that strange girl who had appeared for a few hours, then vanished. *Go on,* she told herself. *Press the button.* But something stopped her. What if she never managed to come back to this place and this time? If she pressed the button on the device, would she be abandoning her brother? She would wait till the last possible moment, she decided, and only return to her own time if her life was actually in danger.

Alfred was issuing orders to his bodyguard, a tall, bearded man who looked as if he had fought many battles before. He had scars along both arms, and probably more under his tunic. His name was Selwyn.

'We will wait for the invaders here,' Alfred said to him. 'We'll hold up the Northmen for as long as we can. If more ships are coming behind the first, we should have enough time to escape before they arrive.'

'Yes, my lord.' Selwyn hurried away to collect weapons and armour.

Alfred turned to Scarlett. 'Come with me,' he said.

He led her back to the hut, where he opened the wooden chest, and took out the two books.

'Take these,' Alfred said. He gave the two books to Scarlett. 'Hide in the trees. Wait there till the battle is over and we've sent them away. Save my books.'

'Why do your books need saving? I thought you were going to *defeat* the Northmen.'

'I hope we will, but who knows what will happen.'

'You're the king's son,' Scarlett told Alfred. 'You don't have to be here. You should run too. Hide. Save yourself!'

'Not before all the villagers have gone,'

Alfred said. 'I need to make sure they're safe.'

'I thought you were meant to be ill,' Scarlett said.

'I'm well enough to fight. Now, please, take these, and go. Hide in the woods. This isn't your battle. Anyway, you're just a girl, you shouldn't be here.'

Scarlett was tempted to do as he said. She could run across the fields and into the shelter of the nearby forest, then continue searching for Thomas. Where would she go? She didn't know. But she'd only come here to find her brother, she didn't want to get waylaid by a battle.

But he'd said she was *just a girl*.

And that really annoyed her.

'I'm staying,' she said.

Alfred didn't waste any time trying to persuade her to leave. He opened the wooden chest again, placed the books inside, and pulled out a short sword, which he gave to Scarlett.

Back at home, if she chopped up a cucumber or an onion, Mum and Dad would fuss around her, making sure she didn't cut off her fingers. *Be careful*, they would say. *Watch what you're doing.* If only they could see her now.

She swung the weapon nervously from side to side, feeling its weight. She'd seen swords in pictures and movies, and in a museum, but never held one in her hand before.

'I don't know how to use this,' she said.

'It's easy,' Alfred replied. 'You stick the sharp end in the other guy.'

12

Bjorn Boatmaker shouted an order to the men in the middle of the boat: 'Bring down the sail!'

Two men stood up, grabbed the ropes, and lowered the sail, which flapped in the wind, jerking this way and that, as if it were a living creature trying to escape from them. They bundled up the material, stowed the sail by the mast, and quickly coiled up the ropes and pulleys.

In this stretch of river, with the wind coming from the side, rather than behind them, the longship's single sail would have been worse than useless, so they relied entirely on the oarsmen for the final approach.

'Come on! Pull harder!' Bjorn's shout came

from the back of the ship. 'We're almost there. Come on! Pull! Pull!'

Thomas turned his head as often as he could, and sneaked a glimpse at the shore, watching the village which came a little closer with every pull of the oars.

 He could see a few small single-storey huts, each with a thatched roof. The walls looked as if they were made of wood and straw. Simple wooden fences penned in some pigs. Goats and chickens were dotted around the fields. Only one thing was missing: people.

'Look!' One of the Vikings pointed at the hillside behind the village. 'They're running away.'

Thomas could see several men, women and children leaving their huts and hurrying across the grass, heading for the shelter of the woods.

'Come back!' Olaf yelled to them. 'Come and fight!'

'Cowards!' shouted another Viking.

The villagers probably couldn't understand what was being shouted at them. But even if they could, they didn't want to waste any breath answering. A couple of them looked back, saw the ship, and sped up, desperate to reach the forest before the Vikings landed.

'Let's get there before they all escape,' Bjorn urged the rowers. 'We want to get some good slaves, don't we? Pull the oars, lads! Pull!'

Godwif was the last to leave.

She was carrying her granddaughter, Judith, tucked into a sling at her side. As a grandmother carrying a tiny baby, she should have been the first to flee from the village and get into the safety of the forest, but she didn't want to run away until she'd persuaded Alfred to escape with her. 'You don't have to fight them, my lord.'

'I do,' Alfred said. 'Otherwise they'll come after you. Hide in the forest. They won't come after you there. They only want to steal whatever they can carry. Go on, Godwif. Look after Judith, don't worry about us. We'll be fine.'

'How can you fight an army?'

'It's not an army, it's just one boat. Go on, take little Judith, keep her safe.'

Reluctantly Godwif turned and hurried after the rest of the villagers. Now the village had only five defenders. One was a seasoned warrior, who had seen many battles, and bore the evidence in scars all over his face and arms. Two more were men from the village, shepherds and farmers, who might have been experts with a scythe or a plough, but barely knew how to use a sword or a spear. And the last two fighters were both children, one of whom had never used a weapon in her life.

The five of them hid in one of the huts, three lurking by one of the windows, two more by another. They all had a good view of the longship approaching the village, but they wouldn't be spotted by any of the invaders.

Alfred had been waiting for a second boat to appear behind the first, or a third, or even

many more, but to his relief, there appeared to be only one.

'That's good,' Alfred told Scarlett. 'We wouldn't have any chance against a thousand men, or even a hundred, but we can defeat twenty.'

Really? thought Scarlett. A boy, a girl, two farmers, and a single warrior against twenty men – surely they wouldn't be able to win

this battle?

As the longship approached the village, Scarlett got a good look at the boat. It must have been fifteen or twenty metres long. Twenty oarsmen sat in the boat, ten on each side, and a single man stood at the back, grasping some kind of tiller with both hands, steering the longship.

Large round wooden shields had been hung

over the sides of the boat. They were brightly painted in different colours and patterns.

The prow was decorated with a fierce dragon, carved from dark wood, its mouth wide open, showing a long tongue and vicious fangs.

According to Alfred, the Northmen had started attacking the Kingdom of Wessex in larger numbers recently, arriving with fleets of twenty or thirty boats, each holding many men. Some of their boats were twice the length of this one and had as many as eighty oarsmen.

'We're lucky,' Alfred said. 'These Northmen aren't an army, just a few thieves and bandits.'

'What if they're friendly?' Scarlett asked. 'What if they've come to trade, rather than rob you?'

Alfred laughed. 'The Northmen are vicious savages,' he said. 'They can't read. They can't write. They worship strange gods. They're not interested in trade, they just want to steal.'

'These ones might be different,' Scarlett suggested. She remembered what she had learned from Miss Wellington and researched for her project: some Vikings had preferred trading to fighting. They were merchants, not warriors. And there had definitely been Vikings who could read and write, although they carved runes on rocks, rather than using books. Maybe Alfred didn't know about them.

'You can't trust the Northmen,' Alfred told her. 'They have been attacking us for years, stealing whatever they can. If we let them, they would take everything that we own. My father, King Althelwulf, thought that God was punishing him by sending these foul beasts to attack us. You know what he did? He decided to send me, his youngest son, to Rome, so I could talk to the Pope. On the way back, I travelled through West Francia, where I met King Charles the Bald.'

'What did you say to them?'

'Not much. I was only five. But they talked to my father's advisers, and promised to send men and weapons to fight against the Northmen.'

'Did they?'

Alfred shook his head sadly. 'No, they did not. They hate and fear the Northmen as much as us, but they only fight to protect their own property. They didn't send a single soldier to Wessex. Not one! If we're going to defeat the Northmen, we'll have to do it ourselves.'

14

'Oars!'

Bjorn yelled that single word at the top of his voice, but he could have whispered, because all the warriors on the boat had been waiting for him to speak. They knew what was coming, and what they had to do. Almost in a single movement, they all lifted their oars out of the water and held them upright, dripping water, then swung them around and tucked them into the bottom of the boat.

Bjorn shouted again: 'Orm, Torsten – go! Go!'

Those two men, Orm and Torsten, had been waiting for his signal, crouching at the very front of the longship. Now they leaped into the waist-deep water, and waded to the shore, carrying coiled ropes.

The villagers had sunk several wooden posts into the mud near the shore, where they could tether their own craft. Two little boats, no bigger than a rowing boat that you might use on a pond, were currently tied to one of the posts.

Orm tied a rope from the ship's prow to the nearest post, and Torsten tied a second rope from the stern to another post.

A storm or a high tide might pick up the longship, snap the ropes, and yank it out to sea, but the river was calm now, and the skies were clear.

Some of the warriors wore leather vests. A few had chain mail. All of them grabbed their weapons, laughing and chatting. Looking at them, Thomas couldn't believe that they were heading into battle, when any of them might lose their lives. They looked more like a group of blokes at a football match, ready to cheer on their team, excited before a big game.

Maybe they wouldn't fight a battle today. Maybe all the villagers had gone. Maybe no one would resist them, and they could steal whatever they wanted, then sail away.

Following the example of the other Vikings, he slid over the side of the boat, plunged into the knee-deep river, and waded ashore. He hardly noticed how cold the water was.

As soon as Thomas reached the grassy shore, he checked his own weapons yet again. The knife fastened to his belt. The shield in his left hand. The small axe in his right. All present and correct. He was ready for battle.

He had never used any of these weapons before, but he was sure it wouldn't be difficult. He'd seen enough movies and played enough games where warriors used spears, axes, and knives. He knew what to do. Stab and slash. Use the shield to defend yourself, or attack with it if you get a chance, whacking your enemy with the reinforced metal hub at its centre.

'Hey, Thomas!' Olaf beckoned. 'Come on!

Thomas reluctantly made his way to the front of the line. He would rather have been at the back, as far as possible from the fighting. But he had been sent by Odin to bring good luck to these adventurers, so he had to march at the front of the column. Together he and Olaf strode across the grass, leading the band of warriors towards the village.

Scarlett stood with Alfred, Selwyn and two villagers, sheltered and hidden in the hut's shadows, peering through the windows, watching the longship approach the shore.

She saw the Viking warriors unhooking their shields from the side of the longship, then sliding into the water, and wading through the shallows to the shore. They laughed and joked like a group of mates enjoying themselves, not a little army preparing for battle.

Weapons in their hands, the line of twenty men came towards the village. Some of them wore leather armour, a couple had chain mail. Some were bare-headed, others had helmets made from metal or leather. All of them were armed with fierce-looking spears, knives, axes, or swords. Here they came, twenty fierce warriors, ready for battle.

Twenty men – and one boy.

He was smaller than the others, and younger, but he held himself with the same confidence and swagger. He was carrying a small axe in his right hand and a shield in his left. He had a leather helmet perched on his head. It must originally have belonged to a man with a bigger head – his father, perhaps – because it didn't fit very well, and kept slipping over his eyes, preventing him from seeing where he was going.

Marching beside him was a huge man. A terrifying warrior who looked as if he could rip you in half. He had a long beard, decorated with beads which glittered in the sunshine, glowing as brightly as the chain mail which covered his chest. He had silver bracelets on both arms, a helmet on his head, and was

carrying an enormous axe.

The biggest warrior and the smallest, striding together at the front of the group, leading them into battle.

Alfred gave an order to the men standing beside him.

'Ready.'

All four of them took up their bows, and drew back the strings, holding them taut. The two farmers might not have fought with a sword or spear before, but they both knew how to use a bow and arrow, having hunted in the woods all their lives.

'Don't shoot until I give the word,' Alfred whispered.

Thomas stared at the village, searching for movement, waiting to see any sign of inhabitants. Had everyone fled? Where had they gone? If they had abandoned the village, what would they have left behind?

He was surprised to see how tatty and worn the houses looked. The thatched roofs needed mending. The walls had holes for windows, but no glass.

A couple of goats looked up at the intruders, then went back to chewing grass.

A dog yapped frantically. He must have been left behind, forgotten by his owners, because he was running around in circles, confused and worried, unsure whether to come and greet these new arrivals, or run away from them.

As they marched closer to the houses, Thomas glimpsed some movement in the shadows of an open window.

Then he heard a pair of strange noises.

A whoosh, followed by a thud.

What could have made that sound?

Alerted by a shout behind him, he turned around, and saw the answer

to his question. The whoosh had been an arrow flying through the air. The thud had been the sound of that arrow thumping into human flesh.

The arrow's head was buried in Bjorn's thigh. The shaft was still quivering from the force of the impact.

For a long moment, Bjorn looked down at the arrow.

Then he said, 'Some idiot just shot me.'

The words had barely left Bjorn's mouth when Thomas heard the same noise again, although this time he recognised it, and knew what would be coming. Another whoosh, another thud. Another arrow had struck one of them. This time the arrow had hit Orm in the chest.

Orm put both hands around the arrow as if he wanted to pull it out of his heart.

Then his knees crumbled beneath him, and

he fell forwards and collapsed on the ground, letting out a little moan of agony.

The noise was repeated again. Twice more. One of the arrows missed them entirely, sailing past and landing in the grass, but the other hit a man in his arm. In a second, Thomas was sure, one of those arrows would hit him.

Assaulted by this fierce rain of arrows, the Vikings could have lifted their shields and formed a defensive barrier. Or they could have turned around and retreated to the safety of their ship.

Instead Olaf lifted his sword. 'Come on,' he yelled to the rest of his friends. 'Let's get them!'

In a mad rush, the Vikings charged towards the village, determined to find the archers who had fired on them.

Bjorn hobbled after them, an arrow still sticking out of his leg. He hadn't bothered removing it. That could wait till after the battle.

One man stayed behind. Orm lay on the ground, not moving. He wouldn't be coming home with the rest of the crew, or taking his share of the treasure.

Along with the others, Thomas found himself shouting and screaming at the top of his voice, although he didn't even know what he was saying. He just wanted to make some noise. To fill his opponents with terror. And forget that he himself felt scared. Luckily he didn't have time to stop and think, because here came the village's defenders, emerging from one of the houses. With wild cries, trying to intimidate their opponents, the two sides threw themselves into the battle. Metal blades thumped against wooden shields. Men swung their axes, lunged with their spears.

Thomas had seen hundreds of vicious conflicts in movies and TV shows, too many to remember, and played games full of blood and gore, where soldiers were shot and stabbed and blown to pieces, but a real battle was somehow very different. When someone died in a game, he just laughed, or forgot it and fired back, pressing the buttons on his controller, but here, surrounded by actual people and real weapons, he felt shocked and sickened by the sights, the smells, and, worst of all, the sounds. The clash of weapons, the crunch of breaking bones. The screams of warriors who had been punched, kicked, slashed, or stabbed.

No time to worry about that now. If he was going to survive, he had to keep fighting. A man was coming towards him, armed with a long sword. He'd never seen anything so shocking, so terrifying. He sprang backwards, and raised his shield, more in a reflex than with a plan to save himself. The sword clanged against the metal boss in the middle of his shield, sending

a fierce impact reverberating down the entire length of his arm. His senses were jangling. He could hardly breathe. He raised his axe — and it was knocked straight out of his hands, and skittered across the grass, out of reach.

He reached for the knife tucked into his belt, but he didn't have time to pull it out before his opponent bore down on him again, whirling his sword through the air.

Thomas staggered backwards, dodging this way and that, trying to escape.

The blade just missed him, but it came so close that he could actually feel the swoosh of its passage through the air.

Opposite him, the warrior raised his sword again, and was just about to take another swipe, the final blow, the killer attack, when he let out a startled cry.

He had been slashed down the length of his spine with an axe. He turned around — and came face to face with Olaf. The big Viking had come to Thomas's rescue. Just in time. He swung the axe again.

Thomas heard the sickening thud of metal meeting flesh. A scream of agony. The man dropped his weapon, fell to the ground, and lay on his back, moaning, writhing. Only a moment ago, this man had been about to kill Thomas, and now he was sprawled on the ground, wriggling away, desperately trying to escape, to save himself.

Olaf gripped his axe with both hands and lifted it into the air.

'No!' Thomas cried instinctively. Of course he was relieved to be alive, but he also felt disgusted, appalled. *Stop now,* he wanted to say. *Leave him alone. Take him prisoner. You don't have to kill him, even if he was trying to kill me.*

With all his strength, Olaf brought the axe

down and buried the blade in the middle of the man's chest, cutting him open. Blood spurted in every direction. The warrior gasped, gurgled, and died.

Thomas turned away. This was different to any movie, any game. This was real. He wished he'd never come here. He should go back to his own time, and ask for Grandad's help, and use the wormhole to return to this place a few minutes in the past, and change things. Make it different. Stop the attack. Save this man. Bring him back to life. He'd never seen anything so awful, so sickening. He didn't want to be here any more. He didn't want to see anyone else suffering or dying. He wanted to go home.

⟨⟨⟨ 17 ⟩⟩⟩

The Vikings won the battle quickly and easily. Of course they did, because they were a horde of ferocious warriors against a man, a boy, a couple of farmers, and a girl who had never taken part in a battle before, never really even fought anyone, unless you counted pushing and shoving her brother in the garden, and that was completely different. They might have kicked one another in the shins, or even swung a few punches, but they'd never picked up a real weapon, never faced the prospect of death.

One of the Vikings had died.

And two of the men from Wessex.

Alfred's guard, Selwyn, lay on the ground, his

125

chest gaping open, his shattered ribs exposed, his blood on the grass. He had fought well, shooting several men with his bow, hacking others with his sword, but the invaders had eventually been too strong for him.

One of the farmers was dead, while the other had managed to escape, dropping his bow at the last moment, dodging through the houses, fleeing across the fields, and sprinting towards the shelter of the forest. He was pursued by a couple of the Vikings, who followed him as far as the trees, then gave up and turned back, deciding that they would never be able to find him in the forest.

Scarlett and Alfred were both unhurt, but they were stunned and upset by the brutality of the battle. They stood at the centre of a circle of Northmen. From listening to their conversation, Scarlett had already learned two of their names. The biggest of them all was named Olaf. Another man had been shot in the battle, and still had an arrow sticking out of his leg; his name was Bjorn.

Then there was the boy. The kid with the helmet too big for him. When he lifted it off, Scarlett saw his face for the first time, and felt a bizarre mixture of shock and joy. She wanted to shout his name, run to him, give him a hug, but he stared blankly at her, offering no sign that he recognised her, merely giving a little shake of his head as if to say, *It's not safe, be careful, let's wait for the perfect moment.*

Scarlett understood. She gave a little nod back at him.

She could have carried on eavesdropping on the Vikings' conversation, gathering useful information, but she chose to let them know that she could speak their language. She asked what they wanted.

'You have a choice,' Olaf said to her, 'you and

your friend.' Meaning Alfred. 'Either you can tell us where you have hidden your treasure, or we'll kill you, *then* take your stuff. Which would you prefer?'

'If we let you take everything, you'll leave us alone? You'll let us walk away?'

'Yes,' Olaf told her.

'Do you promise?' Scarlett asked.

'We promise,' Bjorn said.

All the other Vikings nodded too, giving their agreement.

Alfred looked confused and worried. Scarlett wanted to reassure him. *Don't worry*, she would have said. *You haven't been betrayed. I'm not a spy or a traitor, I can speak their language, and I'm negotiating on your behalf.* But she'd have to wait before giving him an explanation. She was sure he'd be happy, and would agree that she had made the right decision. Once they were free – when she and Thomas had found a way to outwit these Vikings, and the three of them were walking into the woods together, going to find Godwif, Judith and the other villagers – she would explain to Alfred how she was able to speak to the Vikings, and the deal that she had struck with them.

'There's a big wooden chest in that hut.' Scarlett pointed it out. 'You'll find all the treasure in there.'

Four of the Vikings hurried over to the hut. Meanwhile Bjorn fetched a rope, hobbled over to Alfred and Scarlett, and tied them up.

Scarlett was bewildered. 'I thought you were going to release us?'

Bjorn smirked. He looked around at the rest of the Vikings. 'Lads, do you hear that? She *believed* us!' They burst out laughing.

'You can't break your promise,' Scarlett cried out. 'That's just not right!' Her words made the men laugh even harder. She glanced at her brother, hoping he would argue her case, but he gave another quick shake of his head. Maybe he had a plan of his own. If so, she wished he would get a move on.

'What are you going to do with us?' Scarlett demanded.

'We'll take you to the slave market,' Bjorn replied. 'You're both young, fit and healthy — someone will snap you up.'

Alfred was staring angrily at Scarlett. 'How do you speak their language?' he demanded. 'Are you one of them?'

'No, no, I learned it at home,' Scarlett improvised. 'From a slave.'

Alfred could believe that. The villages were full of foreigners. Especially if you lived near the coast. 'What were you saying to them?' he asked.

Scarlett confessed the terrible mistake that she had made. She felt so stupid. She apologised for being such an idiot.

'Now you know,' Alfred said. 'Never trust a Northman.'

The four men emerged from the hut carrying the contents of the wooden chest. They had found a woven shawl, some pots, a couple of knives, some balls of fine wool, a blanket, various clothes, and the two books which had been carefully and lovingly wrapped in fine cloth.

'This is everything,' one of the men said.

'That's it?' Bjorn asked Scarlett. 'Seriously? That's all your treasure? No gold? No silver?'

'Those books are very valuable,' Scarlett said.

'You must be joking.' Bjorn grabbed one of the books. 'We want gold. We want silver. We want weapons. Not this rubbish. I've seen these before. Let me tell you, they're only good for one thing.'

He took the book over to the fire.

'No,' Scarlett called out to him. 'You can't do that!'

'I can do what I want,' Bjorn said.

He dropped the book into the heart of the flames.

The cover browned and warped. The pages crackled. Soon the entire book was ablaze.

That book was – had been – a copy of St Matthew's gospel. Scarlett remembered the beautiful little illustrations of animals, plants and people which had been painted on every page. They must have taken months, even years, of effort by several talented artists. And in a moment, they were gone, reduced to a blackened lump of soot.

'Give me the other one.' Bjorn held out his hand.

'Stop,' Scarlett said again, but this time she knew her words would be ignored.

Beside her, Alfred stared in despair at his most prized possession, his mother's book. He had won it in a contest, defeating his brothers by learning a poem off by heart. And now that beloved book was in the hands of Bjorn, who tore off the cover and tossed it into the fire.

'Please don't do that!' Scarlett said. 'I beg you.'

Bjorn took no notice. He tore out the first page of the book, not even pausing to examine its beautiful decorations, and added the thick sheet to the flames.

For a moment, the page seemed to come alive, as if the words were dancing in the fire. Then it was burning so brightly and quickly that you couldn't even tell what it had once been.

'Stop him,' she hissed at Thomas, but he shook his head again. There was nothing he could do, he was saying with that gesture. He didn't have any control over these Northmen. They would never do what he said.

Bjorn tore the pages out of the book, one by one, adding each of them to the fire. He smiled at the destruction that he was causing. When he got bored, which didn't take long, he threw what remained of the book on the fire, left it to burn, and walked away to search the village for some treasure that he actually wanted.

Scarlett stared miserably at the last scraps of paper curling in the heat and bursting into flame. She glanced at Alfred, and saw that he was bitter rather than sad, his face set with a determined expression. As if he was fixing this moment in his memory. And already plotting how to take revenge.

18

After a battle, you have a feast.

The bigger, the better.

During their voyage, Bjorn, Olaf and the rest of the crew had spent their days and nights exposed to the elements, lashed by the wind and the rain. They had been blown off course by a storm, and rowed until their fingers were covered in blisters, and endured a diet of water and dried meat and stale bread, plus the occasional fish if anyone was lucky enough to catch one over the side of the boat. Today they had won their first battle – so they wanted to celebrate!

They killed two sheep, butchered the carcasses, and put the meat on the fire.

Erik Stargazer found some wooden plates. When the food was done, they shared it out, cutting the meat with their knives, then using their fingers. There weren't any forks. Thomas followed their example, using his fingers to pick up his food, and wiping his greasy hands on his clothes.

They ate the roast lamb with fresh bread, white cheese, raw carrots and radishes, and chopped cabbage. For pudding, they feasted on tiny little strawberries, and handfuls of walnuts and hazelnuts, which some of the men had found carefully stored in one of the huts. All this food might have fed the entire village for days, if not weeks, but the Vikings gobbled it all down in one night.

They raided the village's store of mead, a wine made from honey, and opened all the jars, then tried every one to see which tasted

best. They drank a toast to their dead friend.

'To Orm,' Bjorn said. 'He is on his way to Valhalla. We will join him soon.'

'To Orm,' echoed the others, and they drained their cups.

The Vikings spent a long time telling stories about Orm, remembering the funny things that he had said or done. His acts of bravery. The names of his parents, siblings, wife and children, still waiting for him back at home, not yet aware that poor Orm was dead. They would never see him again; their son, their brother, their husband, their father.

The rest of the men had already patched up their wounds, making simple bandages from cloth. One of the Vikings had lost a finger in the fight, another had received a nasty blow to the head, a third had been stabbed in the elbow, and several had been shot by arrows, but only Orm had lost his life. Erik Stargazer rubbed herbs into their wounds, and bound cloth around their cuts to stop the bleeding. Bjorn had been limping around for hours with an arrow sticking out of his leg, but he finally agreed to lie down, and let Erik cut the arrowhead out of his flesh.

Olaf totted up the numbers. 'Nineteen of us. Plus you, Thomas, which makes twenty. Bjorn gets an extra share for the boat, so that makes twenty-one altogether.'

They were planning to sail to a market, where they would lay out their wares, and sell all the valuables that they had stolen today: the livestock, the weapons, the slaves, and everything else. Then they would divide the profits into twenty-one equal shares.

'What will you spend it on?' Olaf asked Thomas.

'I don't know.'

'Wait and see how much we get,' Erik Stargazer said. 'If you're lucky, and we sell all this stuff for a decent amount, you might be able to buy a knife, or a helmet, or maybe even an axe. You'd only need a small one, you're not a big lad.'

Olaf liked that idea. 'Get some weapons and armour, and stay with us. Carry on raiding. See where we end up. You've brought us good luck so far, just like you said you would. You might not be strong yet, or much of a fighter, but you'll get better, I'm sure of that. You'll have fun with us, I promise.'

'Where are you going next?' Thomas asked.

'Who knows? We'll keep sailing through the summer. Earning what we can. Having a laugh. Then we'll head home in the autumn, once the weather changes.'

Bjorn nodded. 'Stay with us, keeping fighting, and by the end of the summer, you'll have enough to buy a house back home.'

'That sounds fun,' Thomas said with a smile.

He hoped the Vikings were fooled, but the truth was, he couldn't wait to get away.

He wished he could enjoy being here. He still liked Olaf, Bjorn Boatmaker, and the other Vikings, and enjoyed their company, and loved listening to their conversation, but something had changed. He couldn't forget the sight of that warrior, sprawled on the ground, hands in the air, begging for mercy.

He glanced at the two slaves, the boy and the girl, who had been tied up and left in the gloom, not far away. He would have liked to go over there and talk to Scarlett. To reassure her. To promise her that everything was going to fine. *Don't worry,* he would say. *I have a plan. I'm going to rescue you.* But he didn't say any of that, he simply pretended not to know her, to never have seen her before.

Thomas was trying to conceal his real feelings, but Olaf must have noticed that he was looking worried, because he said, 'Why are you looking so gloomy?'

'I'm just thinking,' Thomas said.

'Don't do that! Didn't anyone tell you that thinking is bad for you? It only leads to problems. Have some fun instead. Eat! Drink! Let's sing a song. Or play a game. Tonight is a feast, you have to enjoy yourself!' Olaf drained his cup, and looked around for the jug. 'Lads, I'm thirsty! Pass the mead!'

When the men had eaten so much that they could barely move, they sat around the fire, telling stories, not only about Orm, but also about their own families, their ancestors, and their gods. Thomas was probably the only person who hadn't heard these stories before. The others appeared to know them all well, and nodded at some moments, or sat forward at others, eagerly anticipating the twist in the tale, or the funny moment that would come next.

Skeggi was the best storyteller. He told some funny stories about Loki, the god who played tricks on people and other gods. He described a battle between Odin and Jesus Christ, the god worshipped by the men who lived here in this land; it was only a short fight, because Odin won so easily. He told the tale of a ship's crew who came from another village not far from their own.

'It was the spring,' Skeggi said. 'The snow had melted, the ice had gone, and the men were growing restless for adventure. They sharpened their swords, loaded their ship with provisions, and said farewell to their wives and children. On a day when the wind was good, they set sail for foreign lands.'

These men sailed west, Skeggi explained, past Mercia and Wessex, and past Francia too, following the coast around to the south, pursuing the sun to hotter lands, exploring new kingdoms, travelling all the way to the lands ruled by the Muslims, whose towns had more treasure than you could imagine.

'They gathered so much, they had to leave

most of it behind,' Skeggi said. 'They dug a hole in the ground and buried gold and silver and all kinds of jewels. They sailed home, and feasted until they could eat no more. The following year, when spring came again, they returned to the same place, intending to pick up their gold and silver, but they couldn't find the place, however much they searched.' Skeggi lowered his voice, and glanced from side to side as if he was worried that thieves might be eavesdropping. 'There's a treasure waiting in the earth,' he said. 'Waiting for whoever is lucky enough to dig in that spot . . .'

'We should go there,' someone suggested. 'Get it ourselves.'

'We don't know where to look,' someone else pointed out.

'Some farmer will find it,' Olaf said. 'He'll be ploughing the earth with his oxen, and he'll stumble across a pile of gold and silver so enormous he'll never have to work again.'

'When he does, we'll steal it from him,' Bjorn said, and all the men cheered and applauded.

It was late. Thomas was beginning to doze off, his eyes growing heavy, but he forced himself to stay awake. He needed to be the last man standing. Once the rest of the crew had drifted off, he would sneak over to his sister, release her, and together the two of them would escape. He didn't like the idea of leaving without saying a proper goodbye to Olaf, who had been so kind to him, but what choice did he have? He couldn't exactly say that he was planning to jump through a wormhole and return to the future.

He pulled a small object from his pocket and gave it to Olaf.

'Here,' he said. 'I want to give this to you.'

Olaf took the fidget spinner, and turned it around and around in his enormous hands, trying to work out what it might be. 'What is this?' he asked.

'It's a gift from Asgard,' Thomas said. 'Odin plays with these all the time.'

'I did not know that,' Olaf said. 'Why are you giving it to me?'

'I thought you might like it. Here, this is what you do with it.'

He demonstrated how to use the fidget spinner.

Olaf chuckled. 'I like it,' he said, playing with the toy himself.

Harald Littlebeard had been watching them. 'What have you got there?' he asked.

'Oh, nothing,' Olaf said, and tucked the fidget spinner into the pouch tied to his belt. He gave Thomas a secret smile. 'Thank you,' he said.

'My pleasure,' Thomas said, smiling back, trying to look cheerful, not wanting to give any hint of the sadness and regret that he was really feeling. Tomorrow morning, when the Vikings discovered that he and Scarlett had gone, they would probably be furious, but Olaf might feel differently. He would have the fidget spinner to remind him of Thomas. He could take it back to his own village, and give it to his children, and they could play with it over the long, dark, cold winter.

19

The Northmen's party continued until late into the night.

Scarlett and Alfred had been tethered to one another and to a post, so they couldn't possibly escape. They simply had to sit there, angry and frustrated, listening to the songs, shouting, and laughter echoing around the village in the darkness.

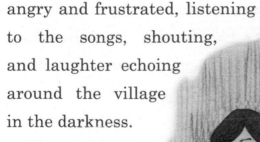

Thomas didn't come near them. He still hadn't spoken to Scarlett.

She felt so angry with him. Why hadn't he rescued her? Why didn't he untie the ropes that had been knotted around her wrists and ankles? Then she could reach into the pouch tied to her belt, and press the button on the device that was still there, tantalisingly out of reach, and they would both be transported to safety.

The only problem was Alfred.

She couldn't leave him here as a slave. That would be a terrible betrayal of her friend.

So should she take him too? Bring him to the future? Imagine the three of them stumbling out of the time machine into Grandad's workshop! Alfred could have a shower, change into some modern clothes, get a lift in a car, visit a supermarket, watch TV – it would be brilliant! She couldn't help giggling. They'd have such fun together. Showing the modern world to a boy from Anglo-Saxon times. He'd learn a lot. He'd definitely stop being such a sexist. When he came back to his own time, brought here in Grandad's machine, he'd make life better for all the girls in his kingdom. Teach them to read. Let them join the army. Together they'd fight the Vikings and change the course of history . . . No, she couldn't do that. Remember what Grandad always said! You can observe the past, but you mustn't interfere.

Alfred was looking at her strangely; he must have been wondering what she might be thinking about, laughing to herself one moment, frowning the next.

Scarlett pretended she was worried. 'Do you think we'll ever get away? Are we going to be slaves for the rest of our lives?'

'Don't worry,' Alfred replied. 'We'll find a way to escape.'

'How?'

'I don't know yet. But we're going to be fine. God is on our side. He hates the Northmen too.

I've been praying to him. I'm sure he's been listening.' He paused as if he was thinking of the best way to phrase his next question 'Do you believe in the one true God? Are you a Christian?'

'I'm not really religious,' Scarlett said. 'I believe in science.'

Alfred didn't know what that meant. He didn't even understand the concept of science. It wasn't something that he had ever heard of. He only knew about religion and magic. 'The Northmen have their gods, but they're not real. They're just silly stories. Jesus Christ is the only real god. You should believe in him too.'

'You should believe in science,' Scarlett said.

'What kind of god is he?' Alfred asked. 'Where is he from?'

'It's complicated,' Scarlett said, not wanting to tell Alfred too much about science, giving him knowledge that he couldn't have.

152

She changed the subject, and asked who might come and rescue them. How about the villagers? Would they return with more weapons or an army?

'I hope not,' Alfred said. 'They should save themselves, not us.'

'If one of the villagers managed to get to your brother's palace, he'd come back here to rescue us, wouldn't he?'

'I hope so,' Alfred replied. 'But I can't imagine the villagers would get to Wintanceaster quickly enough. By the time they've reached my brother, and he's come back here, the Northmen will have taken us away. We'll just have to hope they drink so much tonight they don't wake up in the morning.'

20

'Wakey, wakey!' Olaf clapped his hands. 'Come on, dozy. It's time to get going. You can't snooze all day.'

Thomas sat up and looked around. He couldn't believe it. He must have fallen asleep. The last thing he remembered was sitting by the fire, listening to another of Skeggi's stories, waiting for the rest of the men to nod off. He felt so stupid! He'd missed his best chance to free his sister.

Around him, he could see the remnants of last night's party. The fire was still smouldering. Plates, bowls and empty jugs were scattered on the grass where they had been discarded.

Bjorn Boatmaker was clutching his head.

'Oh, remind me never to drink mead again! It always gives me such a terrible headache.'

'You say that every time we win a battle,' Olaf laughed.

They breakfasted on leftovers from the night before, then went through the village, removing any valuables from the houses. They took anything that they fancied, anything that looked as if it could be sold: sheep, chickens, goats, piglets, a few knives, some cooking pots, jugs and wooden bowls, and all the weapons that they could find. Four of them carried the wooden chest down to the riverbank. Although it was very heavy, they hoped it might be worth a good amount to someone.

Thomas didn't have a chance to free his sister. She and the other prisoner were always surrounded by people. They were loaded aboard the longship and stowed at the front, tied up.

The Vikings left a trail of destruction. Rubbish strewn across the grass. Broken crockery. Gnawed bones. Empty jugs. Smashed furniture. The remains of the animals that they had slaughtered and eaten. And the locals who had died in the fighting, their bodies left where they had fallen, food for rats or crows.

They treated the body of their own comrade very differently. Erik Stargazer and some of the others had been up since dawn, gathering sticks, straw and branches, which they built in a great pile on a patch of empty land between the village and the riverbank.

They laid Orm on the pile of sticks, dressed in his leather helmet and armour. Someone had snapped off the arrow that killed him and cleaned up the wound. They put him on his back, and wrapped his hands around his favourite weapon, a large axe.

Although his wife would never see him again, she would be pleased to hear that he had gone to Valhalla wearing the necklace that she had made for him, a leather cord studded with silver beads and little lumps of amber.

The Vikings gathered around the pyre. Thomas joined them. He understood that this was a very important moment for them all, a final farewell to their dear friend, their comrade, a man who many of them had known for their entire lives.

Thomas suddenly remembered one interesting piece of information from Miss Wellington's class: the Vikings sometimes burned their dead, because they believed that the smoke would carry them more quickly to Valhalla.

Erik Stargazer lit some twigs in the embers of last night's fire, then carried the flames to the pyre and set it alight. The flames spread quickly across the dry sticks, engulfing the

larger branches, crackling and spitting, and soon setting Orm's body alight.

The Vikings stood in solemn silence, watching a column of black smoke spiral into the sky, carrying their dead friend to his final home.

'Goodbye, Orm,' Olaf said. 'Enjoy Valhalla.'

21

Alfred and Scarlett sat at the front of the longship. Their hands had been tied together, and a second rope tethered them to a wooden bench, preventing them from escaping. They sat side by side, watching the Vikings burn their dead comrade.

Scarlett was both fascinated and disgusted. It was so interesting to see the funeral — and so gross! She'd never forget the sight of a dead warrior engulfed by flames, his body blackening . . . Or the smell of roasting flesh . . . She wanted to turn her head away, or close her eyes, or block her nose, but she forced herself to keep watching. She might never have another opportunity to see anything so extraordinary.

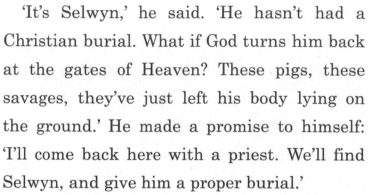

Beside her, Alfred seemed to be angry rather than interested or horrified. She asked what was wrong.

'It's Selwyn,' he said. 'He hasn't had a Christian burial. What if God turns him back at the gates of Heaven? These pigs, these savages, they've just left his body lying on the ground.' He made a promise to himself: 'I'll come back here with a priest. We'll find Selwyn, and give him a proper burial.'

Once their dead friend had been consumed by the flames, the Northmen left the funeral pyre to burn down, and carried on looting the village, grabbing whatever they might be able to sell. They finished loading their booty aboard the longship, then clambered aboard themselves, untied the ropes, launched off, and rowed down the river. As soon as the wind was on their side, they raised the sail, and headed out to sea.

'These guys aren't just nasty, they're stupid too,' Alfred said, looking at the mass of livestock and objects surrounding them, the trussed-up animals, pots and jars, and other bits and pieces looted from the village. 'My books were worth more than all this junk added together.'

'They said they're taking us to a slave market – where would that be?' Scarlett asked him. 'Back to their own country?'

'I don't think so,' Alfred replied. 'More likely, they'll be taking us to Duibhlinn. It has a famous slave market. So does Brycg Stowe, maybe we're heading there. Or they might sail to Rone. Maybe they won't bother sailing as far as a city, they might just head for a market somewhere, or even another village, further down the coast. They'll just be looking for somewhere to sell all this stuff.'

'But it's all stolen! How can they sell it?'

'No one cares where it comes from,' Alfred

explained. 'If the price is low enough.'

'Can't anyone stop them?' Scarlett asked.

'A king could banish the Northmen from our shores,' Alfred said. 'If he raised an army and built a navy.'

'Why doesn't your brother do it?'

'Athelbald? He's too busy worrying about my other brother, Athelberht, the king of Kent. They spend all their time bickering like little kids, rather than joining forces and fighting our real enemy.'

'Maybe you should be king instead.'

'I wish I was,' Alfred said. 'I'd drive the Northmen out of our country.'

He fell silent as they sailed down the river, and into the open sea. He looked back at the hills and cliffs of his own country, shrinking, falling away, gradually disappearing into the distance. He must have been worrying if he would ever see his home again.

Once they were out at sea, the wind picked

up. Dark clouds covered the sky. Soon the storm was upon them. The ropes squealed. One moment, the sail was full of wind, jerking them forwards; the next moment, as the boat tipped and turned, the sail flapped; then it snapped full again, yanking them forwards. Alfred and the Vikings, experienced sailors, weren't concerned, and even seemed to enjoy themselves, but Scarlett hated every lash of wind, every brutal wave, every creak and moan of the timbers. What if the boat fell to pieces? What if they tipped over, laden down with such a heavy cargo? Even if her hands hadn't been tied behind her back, she wouldn't have been able to save herself in this rough sea.

A fierce rain poured down on them. There was nowhere to shelter, so everyone aboard was soaked through. The longship bucked and tumbled over the waves, tipping one way, then the other, always threatening to throw its crew

and cargo overboard. The piglets shrieked, the chickens clucked, the goats bleated sadly, and Scarlett felt so sick, so scared, so miserable, she would give anything for this to be over. She hated boats, she hated the sea, she wanted to be back on dry land. Why had she stepped into that stupid time machine? Why hadn't she stayed at home, comfortable and dry in Grandad's kitchen? She soon decided she wouldn't care if she drowned. Anything would be better than this.

Whenever she looked at Alfred, he gave her

a reassuring smile, but somehow that made her feel even worse. Why wasn't he feeling as terrible as her? Wasn't his stomach turning upside down? Wasn't he terrified?

To her astonishment, her brother looked just as cool and calm as everyone else. He sat with his new best friend, Olaf, the huge Viking warrior, grinning, chatting and laughing as if they were riding a rollercoaster or a big wheel. As if they were having the time of their lives. What was wrong with them? What was wrong with her? Why couldn't she laugh it off like them? Oh, no. Her guts turned over again. Scarlett lurched to the side of the boat, put her head over the edge, and threw up. Hating herself for it, she sniffled and cried, but luckily no one could see, because wave after wave soon splashed over her face, sluicing away the tears and vomit, washing her clean.

⊩⊏ 22 ⊐⊩

By that evening, the storm had passed, although the wind remained brisk, speeding the longship through the waves. Erik Stargazer navigated by the stars and the moon. He had made this journey several times before, crisscrossing the sea between Wessex and West Francia, and he promised they would arrive early in the morning.

In the gloom, Thomas could just make out the silhouettes of his sister and her friend Alfred huddled at the front of the ship. He hoped they were managing to get some sleep.

Thomas spoke to Olaf about them. 'Can't we untie them? They're not going to escape, are they?'

'They might jump overboard.'

Thomas laughed at the thought. 'Why would they do that? We're miles from anywhere! They couldn't possibly swim to shore from here.'

'No, you're right, they'd drown.'

'So why can't we untie them?'

'Because they might still jump overboard.'

'You just said they'd drown!'

'Some prisoners choose to die rather than be a slave for the rest of their lives.'

Thomas knew his sister wouldn't do anything so stupid, and was sure her friend wouldn't either, but he could see there was no point arguing with Olaf.

Perhaps he shouldn't have been able to sleep that night, kept awake worrying about his sister, and the fate that might be awaiting her. But to his shame, he slept particularly well, lulled into a deep slumber by the gentle rocking of the boat. When he next opened his eyes, the sun had risen, the sky was clear, and on the horizon, he could see a slim pale line of hills.

Olaf noticed he was awake. 'There's the coast of Francia,' he said.

Thomas ate a hunk of yesterday's bread with a lump of cheese. Once his sister had woken up, he delivered the same breakfast to her, and took another portion for her friend.

'Why are you feeding the slaves?' Harald Littlebeard asked. 'It's a waste of good food.'

'They'll fetch a better price if they're fit and healthy,' Thomas replied.

'He's right,' Erik Stargazer said. 'You should have thought of that, Harald.'

Harald Littlebeard scowled.

When Thomas handed over the food, he finally got a chance to talk to Scarlett.

'You OK?' he asked.

'Couldn't be better,' Scarlett replied. 'I've always wanted to go on a sailing holiday.'

'Very funny. Let's get out of here. Where's the device? Have you got it?'

'It's in this pouch.'

'I'll have to be quick.' Thomas glanced back at Harald Littlebeard, who was watching them closely. 'We'll hold hands, and I'll press the button.'

'Don't,' Scarlett said. 'We can't leave Alfred here.'

Her friend was dozing beside her.

'Let's take him with us,' Thomas said.

'No. We can't do that either. We have to get him back to Wessex. He's Alfred! *You* know — the king.'

Thomas couldn't remember anything about King Alfred. Had they been taught about him by Miss Wellington? If so, he must have been thinking about something else during that lesson. But he understood that they couldn't take a future king back to their own time. Somehow he would have to think of a different plan.

Harald Littlebeard was still watching him, suspicious of the way he was speaking to Scarlett. Thomas gave him a friendly grin, then returned to his place at the back of the boat, sitting beside Bjorn and Olaf.

They sailed into the mouth of a river, which made a natural bay, a perfect site for a harbour.  The town there was called Carusburc, and consisted of about fifty ramshackle huts and houses, along with a couple of stone buildings, a church and a little fortified castle, where the citizens could shelter if they were attacked by raiders.

Wooden posts had been buried in the mud,

171

so you could tie up your boat, and wade ashore at low tide, or row back and forth at high tide. There were as many boats as houses, if not more. Farmers had arrived, bringing carts laden with produce. The market was in full swing. Traders had laid out their wares on the ground. Delicious smells came across the water from stalls where people were selling grilled meat.

As the longship neared Carusburc, two of the Vikings stood at the prow with their arms by their sides, their heads bare, their hands empty, to show that they had come to trade, not to rob. They had wrapped the dragon in a blanket, another sign that the longship was here for peaceful reasons, not sailing into battle.

The citizens of Carusburc had been raided on many different occasions by many different thieves and bandits, so the merchants and farmers now paid a tax to a local warlord, who brought a few of his men here to guard the port.

A large force could easily have overwhelmed these guards, but not a single longship.

The guards waved the longship into the harbour. One of them pointed out a good place to moor. Once the Vikings had tied up their boat, another of the locals came over to talk to them, a man who could speak their language.

'Good morning, and welcome to Carusburc,' he said. 'This is a free market. You can buy and sell whatever you want, but no fighting, please. Settle your disputes elsewhere. We're only interested in trade here, not warfare. And no thieving, do you understand?'

'Don't worry,' Skeggi replied. 'We know the rules, we've been here before.'

The guard asked where they had come from, what they were selling, and if there was anything that they were particularly hoping to buy.

'We're crossing over from Wessex,' Torsten replied. 'We have a few goods to sell. We need to buy some food and weapons, nothing special.'

Bjorn Boatmaker had a request: 'I need someone who can sew up the hole in my breeches. Can you recommend anyone?'

'Try Margot by the bakery,' the local suggested. 'She can mend anything.'

The Vikings moored their longship, found a space in the market, and laid out their wares, showing off everything that they had stolen from the village in Wessex: knives and arrowheads, jugs and bowls, glass bottles, bracelets, beads, a few axes, some rope, chairs, stools, the wooden chest, some sheep and goats, a few chickens, eight little piglets, and two slaves, fit young children, a boy and a girl.

Bjorn Boatmaker wanted to go straight to the bakery and find the woman who would be able to mend his breeches. He showed everyone the hole. 'Look where that idiot shot me yesterday.'

'I need a new helmet,' said Skeggi. 'Mine is falling to pieces.'

A third man wanted to buy some cheese, having heard stories about the amazing stuff that they made here in West Francia. A fourth had toothache and wanted to find a witch or a medicine man who could make it go away.

The Northmen left Torsten and Harald Littlebeard to guard the merchandise and sell their goods to any merchant who was willing to pay a decent price for some wooden bowls, a plump chicken, or a young slave. Torsten spoke the local language, which was why he ran the stall, but Harald Littlebeard didn't understand why he had to stay behind too.

'It's not fair,' Harald complained. 'I should be allowed to have some fun!'

'Stop moaning,' Olaf said. 'You can have a

walk around later. You'll get your chance.'

'I don't mind staying here,' Thomas said. Left with Scarlett and Alfred, he might get a chance to free them. 'You enjoy the market, Harald.'

'You're coming with us,' Olaf told Thomas. 'You bring me good luck, and I'm going to need it. These Francians drive a hard bargain.'

Thomas protested, arguing that he would much rather guard the slaves, but Olaf insisted.

Harald Littlebeard sighed and folded his arms. He gave Thomas a dirty stare. As if to say, *This is all your fault.*

It's really not, Thomas wanted to tell him. *I tried to stay here, I'd much rather be with my sister. You should blame Olaf, not me.* But he didn't say a word, he just smiled at Harald Littlebeard as if they were mates, then hurried after the rest of the crew.

The market was busy. Traders had come from near and far, local farmers mingling with merchants from villages upriver or along the coast, and a great crowd bustled around, buying snacks, knocking back drinks, examining all the goods on offer.

The two children were inspected by traders who were looking for slaves to buy cheaply here, then sell at a different market for a higher price, and by farmers, who wanted slaves to work in their fields and orchards. People checked their teeth, peered into their ears, and prodded their muscles. Alfred and Scarlett tried to look weak, unhealthy and foul-tempered, and it must have worked,

because no one bought them.

Alfred talked to everyone who passed by, asking them questions, until he found a local who spoke his own language. 'Where are we?' he asked. 'What country is this?'

'You're in Carusburc in West Francia,' the man replied. He was a farmer who frequently traded goods across the sea, which was why he spoke the language of Wessex. Today he was wandering through the market with his wife and children.

Alfred asked: 'Charles the Bald – he's still your king, isn't he?'

'Of course,' the man said.

'I've stayed with King Charles in his palace. Please will you send a message to him right away. Tell him that my name is Alfred, I am the son of King Athelwulf, and I need his help.'

The man nodded solemnly. 'I'll go and tell the king right away. I'm sure he'll come here immediately when he knows a slave boy wants to speak to him.' He burst out laughing. His wife did too. Even the three children giggled.

'This isn't a joke,' Alfred protested, but the farmer and his family were already wandering away.

Later, two more merchants strolled past, chatting in a language that Alfred understood. He was delighted – they were men from Wessex.

'Where are you from?' he asked.

They stared at him, surprised to be addressed so familiarly by a slave.

'We're from Holeweye,' one of the merchants said.

'It's a village on Wit,' explained the other.

'I have never been to Holeweye, but I have visited Shamblord,' Alfred said. 'Your island is a beautiful place.'

'It is,' agreed the merchant.

Both he and his companion were still surprised that this slave boy not only spoke so eloquently, but had visited their home, a large island not far from the mainland. They came from a small village on the east side of the island, and often sailed across the sea to West Francia, buying and selling at the markets.

Alfred said, 'When you sail home to Wit, will you take me too? Or even better, to Hamwic?'

The merchants refused. 'Sorry, kid. We're not in the market for slaves. We're here to sell sheep and buy cheese.'

'If you take me to Wintanceaster, I'll buy you enough cheese to fill your boat.'

'If you're so rich,' one of the merchants said, 'why are you a slave?'

'My name is Alfred, I am the son of King Athelwulf. One of my brothers is King Athelbald of Wessex. The other is King Athelberht of Kent. You've heard of them, haven't you?'

Of course they had. One of those men was

their king now, and Athelwulf had ruled Wessex for many years. They even knew the name of Alfred, King Athelwulf's youngest son, although neither of them had ever seen him, so they had no idea what he looked like.

One of them said, 'Where's your brother, the king? Is he here too?'

'No, he's in Wintanceaster.'

'Let's hope he comes and rescues you soon.'

'He would – if he knew I was here!'

'Who are you really, boy? Where are you from?'

'I've told you. My name is Alfred, and I am the son of King Athelwulf, and the brother of King Athelbald. If you take me back to Wessex, I will make sure you are given a good reward.'

Unfortunately the merchants didn't believe him. They thought he was a farmer's son with a vivid imagination. They wished him the best of luck, then walked on.

Thomas went to the bakery with Olaf, Bjorn and Erik Stargazer. They found Margot, who was an old woman armed with several needles made of forged iron or carved bone, threads of different thicknesses, and a bowl filled with buttons and beads. She couldn't speak their language, but Erik could say a few words in hers, enough to explain what Bjorn wanted, and negotiate a fee.

By making gestures, the old woman told Bjorn to take off his breeches.

Thomas was interested to discover that Vikings didn't wear underpants.

The old lady did a brilliant job. The breeches were as good as new, and maybe even better.

Bjorn paid her what they had agreed. Then the four of them had a look around the market together.

Some of locals just had a few vegetables or some fruit for sale: a couple of carrots, some onions, a bunch of herbs. Others sold milk, cheese, or yoghurt. One woman offered pots of honey. Another had bowls of hazelnuts, almonds, and walnuts, which had been dried over the winter, and were now ready to eat.

There were chickens for sale, trussed up or confined in wooden cages, pecking unhappily at the bars. A man sat on the grass with three dead rabbits laid out by his feet. Another had a couple of pigeons.

You could buy furniture or blankets, jewellery and ornaments, scarves and sandals, woollen hats and leather helmets.

They stopped to look at a collection of knife blades and arrowheads. They inspected various fish for sale, and some whale blubber, and several bones which the stallholder claimed had originally belonged to a mermaid.

Hunters and farmers had come to the town from surrounding hills, forests, and villages, bringing whatever they had grown or caught. Merchants and warriors had sailed here from much further away, some coming from the villages up river, others sailing around the coast. Olaf and Bjorn met other groups of Northmen in the market, some from a village only a few miles from their own. One group was intending to sail around the coast of Francia to the Kingdom of Navarre and beyond.

'There is a land in the south ruled by Muslims,' one of them said. 'That's where we're heading. They're so rich, even the slaves are tied up with gold chains.'

'Don't lie,' Bjorn said.

'It's true! I was there myself five years ago. The town is called Ishbiliyah, and it is richer than you can imagine. Even the poorest citizens have fresh water and all the food that they can eat. And the richest – they have so much gold and silver, so many glittering jewels, they won't even notice if you steal a boatload or two!'

'What rubbish,' Bjorn said.

But Olaf believed it. 'Remember what Skeggi told us? Remember the buried treasure? Maybe we'll find it ourselves.'

'You shouldn't believe everything Skeggi says,' Bjorn replied.

The Northman reached into one of the leather pouches tied to his belt. He lifted out his closed fist and opened it to reveal a palm spotted with silver coins. 'You see? These are dirhams, what the Muslims call their money. Come with us and you'll have enough of these to keep you comfortable for the rest of your life. We could do with more warriors. You can have an equal share of the loot. You'll go home with so much gold and silver, you'll need to steal a bigger ship to hold it all.'

Bjorn wasn't convinced. 'Even if we joined forces, we'd only have a few men, not an army. We couldn't attack a town, we'd be slaughtered. We should stick around here and rob a few more villages. Don't get carried away.'

However, Olaf was more enthusiastic. 'We'll be fine! We've got Thomas, haven't we? He brought us luck in the battle like he said he would.'

'He wasn't so lucky for Orm,' Erik pointed out.

'Odin wanted Orm in Valhalla,' Olaf replied cheerfully. 'The rest of us were lucky, weren't we?'

'I got shot in the leg,' Bjorn said.

'Oh, stop fussing. It was just a little arrow. You're fine now, aren't you? Maybe if Thomas hadn't been there, bringing you luck, you'd have been shot in the head instead.'

'Maybe,' Bjorn said.

'He'll bring us luck wherever we go,' Olaf insisted. 'With Thomas on our side, we'll defeat the Muslims, steal their gold, and go home rich.'

'We'll be leaving as soon as the wind is with us,' the Northman said. 'Come with us, you won't regret it.'

Bjorn, Erik, and Olaf promised to think about it. Perhaps they would go south, and see the kingdoms of the Muslims. Or perhaps they would sail back to Wessex, and rob a few more villages, then come here again to sell whatever they had stolen. They couldn't decide for the whole crew. Tonight, they would build a fire, eat some tasty Francian food, drink a few jugs of the local wine, and discuss where to sail next, then take a vote.

'What do you think?' Olaf asked Thomas. 'Will you come a-viking with us? Will you bring us more good luck?'

'I'd like that,' Thomas said.

'Good lad.' Olaf clapped him on the back. 'Now, have you seen anything you want? You'll get your share soon – what are you going to buy? A decent knife? A cosy blanket? Or are you going to save up for something better, an axe, maybe, or a helmet?'

Thomas had been thinking about exactly that. 'I would like to buy those two slaves,' he said. 'The ones we brought with us from Wessex.'

Olaf was puzzled. 'Why do you want them?'

'Odin wants me to buy them,' Thomas said.

Olaf discussed this surprising idea with Bjorn and Erik, who were dubious about the idea. Apart from anything else, they weren't sure of the value of the slaves. Surely they must be worth a lot more than a twenty-first share of their loot? Anyway, why did Thomas want them?

'We should have a vote,' Bjorn suggested.

The other warriors were scattered around the market, and gathering them together would have taken ages. Thomas insisted that he needed to buy the slaves right now.

'Let him have a slave,' Olaf said. 'Go on, give the kid what he wants.'

They discussed it on their walk back to the stall, where they found that Torsten and Harald Littlebeard had managed to sell several of their items for a good amount. The wooden chest had earned more than they had imagined. Alfred's sword and Selwyn's weapons had been worth a lot too. No one had yet made an offer for the two slaves.

'No one wants them,' Harald said. 'She's too grumpy. He's too puny and pale. Neither of them looks as if they've done a decent day's work in their lives.'

That convinced Bjorn and Erik.

'Which one do you want?' Bjorn asked Thomas.

'I want them both,' Thomas said.

'You definitely can't have both,' Erik Stargazer told him. 'Even by giving you one, we're letting you have a great deal.'

Thomas pleaded and begged, but they wouldn't change their minds. Even Olaf agreed that he couldn't possibly buy two slaves with a twenty-first share, that would simply be unfair on the rest of the crew.

'Be happy with what you've got,' Olaf recommended.

Thomas felt so frustrated. If only he had something to sell. Something that would be worth another share. His clothes? His shoes? Or should he stay with Olaf and the Vikings for another voyage, another raid, and earn some more money? No, he couldn't do that, because the Vikings were determined to sell both their slaves before embarking on another raid.

It was an almost impossible decision, but Thomas knew what he had to do: take Alfred to safety first, then come back for his sister. 'I'll take the boy,' he said.

Olaf, Bjorn, and the other Vikings agreed that this was a sensible decision. Boys were usually more valuable than girls – even skinny, sickly boys like this one, with his little muscles and pasty skin.

Thomas untied the rope that bound Alfred to Scarlett. 'Time to go,' he said.

Alfred rubbed the red, raw rings on his wrists. 'Where are you taking me?'

'To find a way to get you back home.'

Scarlett had overheard the end of the conversation between Thomas and the Vikings, and picked up what was going on. She'd understood that her brother had a plan.

Now she reassured Alfred. 'He'll get you back to Wessex,' she promised her new friend. 'You can trust him. He's my brother.'

Now Alfred was really confused. 'If he's your brother, what's he doing with *them*?' Meaning the Vikings.

'They raided our village a few months ago,' Scarlett said. 'Thomas disappeared then. We thought he had been killed, but it turns out they took him prisoner. He managed to persuade them that he would fight on their side.'

Alfred seemed to be convinced by this story. He must have understood that people will do anything to survive. Even work with the enemy. Of course he had many more questions, but Scarlett told him that there wasn't time to answer them. They had to move quickly – before the Vikings changed their mind, or realised that their prisoner was much more valuable than they could have imagined.

'Thank you,' Alfred said to Scarlett. 'Don't worry, I'll find you, wherever you are. I'll be back to rescue you. With an army.'

'Forget about me,' Scarlett said. 'My brother has a plan. Once he's found you a way to get home, he'll get me out of here. I'll be fine, I really will, you don't have to worry.'

Alfred wasn't sure whether to believe her, but Thomas and Scarlett both reassured him that they didn't need his help. He should return to Wintanceaster, they said, and live his own life, and let them lead theirs.

'I hope we'll see one another again,' Alfred told Scarlett.

'I hope so too.'

'Next time you're in Wessex, come and find me.'

'If I'm ever in Wessex again, I will,' she promised.

Almost everything had been sold. The other men had taken their share of the loot and gone to buy provisions or weapons. Torsten and Harald Littlebeard had been left behind to sell the last few bits and pieces: three empty barrels, two knives, a jug of mead, some wooden bowls, and a single chicken, clucking loudly, probably annoyed that it hadn't been given any food all day – and a girl, who was sitting on the ground, legs crossed, arms folded.

'Try to smile,' Harald Littlebeard pleaded. 'No one will want to buy you if you look so grumpy.'

Scarlett stuck her tongue out at him.

She was worried about Thomas. Why was he taking so long? What if he took hours to find a boat that would take Alfred home, and by the time he got back, she'd been sold? How would he ever find her again?

Scarlett wished she could have had a bit more time to say goodbye to Alfred. She still couldn't quite believe that he would grow up to be king – and not just any king, but a king who was remembered hundreds, thousands, of years in the future.

She'd never met a king before. Or anyone who would become a king. The funny thing was, she'd really liked him, and she knew he liked her too. They could have been great friends. If only she could have said a proper goodbye. She thought of all the things she should have said. She knew she wouldn't ever see him again.

Two women wandered past.

'Do you want buy a slave girl?' Torsten asked them.

The women looked at Scarlett, who stuck her tongue out at them too.

'No, thank you,' one of the woman said. 'But how much is that barrel?'

'What are you offering?' Torsten asked.

'I'll give you a bag of apples. They're nice and juicy.'

'This barrel is worth more than a few apples.' Torsten pointed at a beautifully carved bone pin which was pinning up the woman's long brown hair. 'Give me that too, and you've got a deal.'

The woman pulled the pin out of her hair, which fell down around her face, and handed it over. She and her friend tipped the barrel on its side, and rolled it away. Torsten happily put the pin in his pouch, a present for his wife, and took a bite from one of the apples.

Thomas and Alfred walked through the harbour, asking each of the crews where they would be sailing next. Thomas did most of the talking, because the translator allowed him to speak to anyone. Most of the boats were staying nearby, nipping along the coast of West Francia. One was heading to Bretagne, which Thomas thought would be perfect, until he realised that the word meant 'Brittany' not 'Britain'.

'Those guys are from Wessex.' Alfred pointed out two merchants who were untying their boat and preparing to leave the harbour. 'I talked to them earlier, and told them who I was, but they wouldn't believe me.'

'Let's try them again,' Thomas said. He asked the merchants to take Alfred with them. They shook their heads and chuckled, recognising him as the farmer's boy who had pretended to be a king's son. Thomas said, 'How much would you charge for a voyage from here to Hamwic?'

'That depends,' said one of the men.

'On what?'

'What you're offering,' the other man said. 'What have you got? Eggs? Cheese? Chickens?'

'How much would you charge in money?' Alfred said.

The men weren't sure. They didn't often use coins. Occasionally one of them would come into possession of a coin stamped with the king's face, but usually they bought and sold with goods, not money.

'We'll take you from here to Hamwic for two silver pennies,' one of them said.

Thomas looked at Alfred to check the price. He nodded.

Thomas said, 'When are you leaving?'

'Right now.'

'It's a deal.'

The merchants had one more request before they would let Alfred aboard their boat. 'You have to pay half in advance. A penny now, a penny when we arrive.'

'He'll pay you the full amount when you get there,' Thomas said.

The merchants didn't like that idea. 'Half now, half on arrival. That's the deal.'

The skinny boy drew himself up to his full

height. 'I am Alfred, son of Athelwulf, brother of Athelbald, and I promise you, I will pay you whatever I owe you. I give you my word.'

'That's all very nice,' the merchant replied, 'but I can't eat words.'

Thomas came up with a suggestion to clinch the deal. 'How about this? If he's telling the truth, he'll pay you two silver pennies when you deliver him to King Athelbald's men in Hamwic. If he's lying, and he's not really who he says he is, then you can keep him as a slave. You can sell him. Or he'll work for you. For free.'

The two merchants couldn't see a flaw in the deal. Either they earned two silver pennies, which was a good fee for carrying a passenger across the sea. Or they would get a free slave. They ushered Alfred aboard.

'Thank you,' Alfred called to Thomas. 'I'm serious about seeing you and Scarlett again. Come and visit me in the palace in

Wintanceaster. You're both welcome to stay as long as you like. As guests of the royal household. We can hunt together. Build an army. Fight the Northmen.'

'That sounds fun,' Thomas said. 'Maybe we will.'

Thomas waited for a moment, watching the two merchants loading their boat, then untying the ropes, picking up their oars, and heading out to sea. He would have liked to stay there until Alfred was out of sight, but he had to get back.

He rushed through the market. He was almost too late. He could see a man talking to Harald Littlebeard and Torsten, handing over a large triangle of white cheese and several round brown loaves. Scarlett was standing nearby, her hands still tied behind her back. She looked seriously worried and scared. When she saw him, her relief was obvious.

Thomas said, 'What's going on?'

Harald Littlebeard and Torsten both grinned at him.

'Hello, mate,' Torsten said. 'We've finally sold this slave.'

Harald Littlebeard added, 'She's so grumpy, we thought we were going to be stuck with her for ever.'

'She's worth more than some bread and cheese!' Thomas said angrily.

'It's tasty cheese,' Harald Littlebeard said.

'Good bread too,' Torsten added. 'Here, try some.'

Thomas protested, but the deal had been done. The farmer had delivered his bread and cheese. Now he grabbed Scarlett and led her away. She tried to resist, but she wasn't strong enough.

Thomas ran after them. 'Get off her,' he snarled.

'She's mine,' the farmer said. 'I just bought her. Leave me alone.'

'Only if you let her go.'

'She's nothing to do with you, she's my slave now. I paid good cheese for her.'

'Let her go!' Thomas insisted. He grabbed Scarlett, and pulled her towards him.

'Hey! That's my property.' The farmer took a swing at Thomas's head.

Thomas ducked, dodged backwards, then threw himself forwards, both hands raised, and gave the farmer a good strong shove in the middle of his belly.

'Arghhh!' The farmer gave a wild shriek. He stumbled backwards, tripped over the edge of the bank, slithered down the mud and fell into the river with a splash. He stood up, spitting water, and shouted a stream of furious insults at Thomas, promising to take terrible revenge.

People turned their heads to see what was going on. Guards came running. They had wooden truncheons.

'This is a peaceful market,' one of the guards

called out. 'No fighting allowed!'

Torsten and Harald Littlebeard had been watching this in amazement. Now they started yelling furiously at Thomas.

'What are you doing?'

'What's wrong with you?'

'That guy bought our slave!'

'We've been trying to get rid of her all day.'

'He's not buying my sister,' Thomas said.

'Your *sister*?'

The two Vikings stared at him in astonishment.

'We thought you were one of us,' Torsten said.

'I was,' Thomas said. 'Till you made my sister into a slave.'

Torsten and Harald Littlebeard looked at one another, then both nodded. Enough talking, time for action. Vikings didn't waste time arguing when they could be fighting. Torsten reached for a spear, while Harald

grabbed the knife that he always carried slung from his belt.

Scarlett yelled at her brother. 'The device! It's here! In this pouch!'

Thomas grabbed the pouch hanging from her belt, reached inside, and pulled out the device. He looked into his sister's eyes. 'Are you ready?'

'Stop talking so much! Press the button!'

Thomas put his arm through Scarlett's,

linking them together, and pressed the button on the device.

Nothing happened.

He looked up.

Guards were coming from every direction. The farmer was stomping out of the river, his clothes dripping wet, his face contorted with rage. Harald Littlebeard was approaching them, knife in hand, with Torsten just behind.

Harald raised his arm. Lifted his knife.

Thomas whirled around, putting himself in front of his sister, turning his back on Harald Littlebeard, protecting Scarlett.

He braced himself for the impact. The agony as the blade sliced through his flesh.

But it never came, because at that very moment, the wormhole sucked up the twins, spinning them through the time and space.

⫸ 27 ⫷

Scarlett and Thomas stumbled out of the time machine together. They were back where they had started. In their grandfather's workshop.

Grandad hadn't moved. He was standing in exactly the same spot he had been when Scarlett stepped into the time machine.

With a cry of joy, Grandad jumped forward and embraced them both. 'You're safe! This is wonderful!'

Then he wrinkled his nose.

'Blimey, you smell terrible.'

'Nice to see you too, Grandad,' Thomas said.

Scarlett wanted to know one thing. 'How long were we gone for? How much time has passed here in the present?'

'Less than a second,' Grandad said. 'You stepped into the machine and straight out again.'

He took a long look at his two grandchildren. There was something different about them, although he wasn't sure what. They might only have been gone for an instant, but they had both changed. Their faces were filthy. Their clothes too. And there was something else . . .

'Scarlett, why are your hands tied behind your back?'

'It's a long story,' Scarlett said.

'I can't wait to hear it,' Grandad said. 'Once I've done this.'

He hurried over to his control panel, and switched off the machine, powering down the wormhole.

'It's not safe to leave it on full power for too long,' Grandad explained. 'A wormhole is very unpredictable. And dangerous. You never know what might happen.'

'Dangerous?' Scarlett repeated.

'Unpredictable?' Thomas added.

'Grandad!' they both said at the same time.

'You're both perfectly safe, aren't you?' Grandad gave them a cheerful smile. 'Not missing any limbs? No? I thought not. Now, I need to know exactly what happened.' He opened his laptop, and created a new document, ready to write notes on every part of the twins' experience. 'Tell me everything,' Grandad said. 'I want to know if you had any problems, any issues. Any suggestions for improvements? Any tweaks to the technology? Where did the wormhole spit you out? Did you end up in the same place at the same time, or different places at different times? Tell me precisely what you saw and how you felt. From the moment that you arrived in the past till the moment that you returned to the present.'

Thomas shook his head. 'Sorry, Grandad, I can't waste any time talking. I've got to finish my homework.'

'Your homework?' Grandad couldn't believe it. 'Who cares about your homework? I need to hear about my machine! What works? What doesn't work? How am I going to make it even better? Tell me everything!'

But his grandchildren didn't have time to talk to him. They were much too busy. They had so much information about the Vikings swirling around their minds, they wanted to write it all down while it was fresh.

Back in the kitchen, Thomas fetched some scissors from a kitchen drawer and cut the ropes binding Scarlett's hands. She rubbed her wrists. 'Thanks for saving me,' she said. 'For a moment back there, I thought you might have forgotten about me. I thought you might have decided to spend the rest of your life with the Vikings.'

'I was tempted,' Thomas admitted.

'What made you change your mind?'

'Dunno.' Thomas didn't want to have a soppy conversation about missing his sister or how much he cared about her. He just wanted to get on with the day. 'Do you want to have the first shower? Or shall I?'

'Rock, paper, scissors?'

'Sure.'

Scarlett won best of three, and raced upstairs to have a shower. She folded up her tunic. She wanted to take it home as a memento. Before Mum and Dad came to pick them up, she'd have to think of a way to explain what had happened to her jeans and T-shirt. Would she admit that they were currently rolled up and hidden in an Anglo-Saxon village, hundreds of years in the past?

Thomas looked at the familiar surroundings

of his grandfather's house, and realised he was very relieved to be back here. He still felt shaken by the events that he had just experienced, especially the battle in the village, and the violent death of the man who had attacked him. He knew he would never forget the sight of that soldier dying. His panic. His pain. The sound made by Olaf's axe, smacking into the middle of his chest, snapping his ribs. Thomas would be able to hear that vile noise echoing around his mind for the rest of his life, he felt unpleasantly sure of that.

'I'm done,' Scarlett called down to him. 'Your turn.'

After the twins had both showered, they borrowed some of Grandad's clothes, ate several pieces of toast slathered with chocolate spread, and returned to their projects.

They were still writing when their parents came to pick them up. Mum and Dad were surprised and delighted to see their children working so hard.

'Have you had a good day?' Mum asked.

'It's been brilliant,' Scarlett said with a cheerful smile, not wanting to give a hint of what had really happened.

'That's great,' Dad said, 'What have you been doing?'

'Nothing special,' Thomas replied. 'Mostly homework.'

Mum said, 'Why are you both wearing Grandad's shirts?'

Scarlett and Thomas looked at one another. It was a good question – but neither of them could think of a good answer. Luckily, Grandad chose that moment to come into the kitchen and ask who would like a nice cup of tea.

◄═ 28 ═►

On Monday morning, Thomas and Scarlett delivered their projects to their teacher, Miss Wellington. That Friday, they got them back, along with some comments.

Miss Wellington was very pleased with Scarlett's project, although she was a bit surprised by the tone of her work.

'I'm not sure you really liked the Vikings,' Miss Wellington said.

'That's because they were horrible,' Scarlett said. 'They were thieves. They were murderers. And they kept slaves!'

'So did the Anglo-Saxons,' Miss Wellington pointed out.

That was true, Scarlett had to admit.

215

Even King Alfred had allowed his people to keep slaves. She'd been reading about him, discovering how her friend had grown up and what he had done in the rest of his life. He had become king; he had driven the Northmen out of Wessex; and he'd insisted that all the boys in his kingdom learned to read and write. But not the girls. She felt annoyed with him about that. Had he forgotten their conversation?

Once Miss Wellington had handed back everyone's homework, she said, 'I'm very proud of you all. I'm so impressed by your hard work. Well done. I wish I could give a prize to everyone. But in the end, I decided one of you had really excelled. So, without any more ado, I can tell you that the winner of this term's prize for best history project is . . . Thomas!'

Everyone clapped and cheered – including Scarlett. For once, she didn't mind not coming top of the class. Her brother's project *was* amazing. He'd written eight pages of

text, packed with fascinating details. His illustrations were brilliant too. He had drawn a map to show the routes taken by the Vikings, going east to Ukraine, Russia, and Turkey, west to Britain, Ireland, France, and Spain, and across the Atlantic to Iceland, Greenland, and the east coast of North America.

On the cover of his project, Thomas had drawn a Viking warrior, ready for battle, clad in chain mail, holding a round shield and a large axe. He looked ferocious, but he was grinning cheerfully. Only Scarlett recognised him as Olaf.

Miss Wellington said, 'Congratulations, Thomas. Your project is absolutely brilliant. I especially loved your description of sailing in a Viking longship. It was so vivid, so real, I felt as if I was actually there.'

Thomas was delighted. He'd never won anything before. Scarlett was the prizewinner in the family. That was what everyone always said, anyway.

Miss Wellington asked Thomas to go and show his work to the head teacher.

'This is wonderful,' the head said, turning the pages of Thomas's project. 'I can see why you won the class prize. Congratulations.'

'Thanks,' Thomas said.

The head said, 'Can I ask you something?'

'Sure.'

'I hope you don't mind me saying so, Thomas, but you don't always work so hard, do you? What was so interesting about this particular project? What inspired you to put in so much effort and energy?'

Thomas wasn't sure how to answer. Obviously he couldn't admit where he had been and what he had seen. Instead he shrugged his shoulders. 'It was fun, I guess.'

'So you like the Vikings?'

'Oh, yes,' Thomas said. 'I love the Vikings.'

HISTORICAL NOTE

The Vikings didn't actually call themselves 'Vikings'. For them, that word was a verb, not a noun. You weren't a Viking; you went a-viking, which meant sailing to a neighbouring village or a foreign country, stealing their stuff, and coming home rich. Their fearful opponents would have called them 'Northmen'.

Like Olaf and his friends, the earliest Northmen went a-viking in small groups, just a few fighters in a single ship, or a little group of two or three longships, all from the same village or area. They might nip around the coast and raid a few villages or farms; or they would sail further away, heading east or west, hunting, sailing around the coastline, up rivers, across the sea. They would usually set sail in the spring, after planting their crops. They would be back in time to reap the harvest later in the year.

There were many Northmen who behaved differently. Some of them preferred not to fight at all, instead farming or trading. Some swore allegiance to a king or a lord, sailed in fleets of many longships, and fought in big armies,

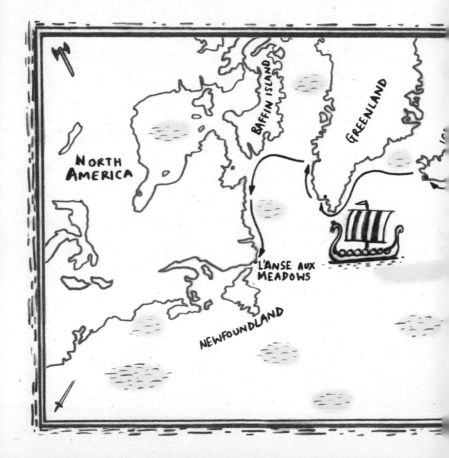

raiding other countries. Some conquered kingdoms, settling in new lands, and starting families, whose descendants might still live in the same territory today.

The first recorded Viking attack in England was in Dorset in 789, when three longships landed near Portland. An Anglo-Saxon man named Beaduheard came to greet them. We

don't know if he was coming to say hello, asking them to pay a tax, or ordering them to go away. He didn't live long enough to tell anyone, because the Northmen killed him on the beach.

Vikings looted the monasteries on Lindisfarne in 793 and on Iona in 795. Over the next couple of hundred years, the Northmen continued their raids throughout Europe, making both small attacks with a boat or two, and much larger invasions with dozens of ships carrying large armies. Various Northmen travelled vast distances, sailing as far as the cities that are now called Baghdad, Kyiv, Istanbul, Granada, Seville and Dublin; they also reached Iceland, Greenland, and the coast of North America, visiting what is now Canada and the USA.

This story is set in 859, when Alfred was probably ten years old. (No one knows exactly when he was born.) As he tells Scarlett, he never expected to become king. Not only was he often unwell as a child, and might not have been expected to survive into adulthood, but he was the youngest of six children with four elder brothers and an elder sister.

After the deaths of his father and brothers, Alfred was crowned King of Wessex in 871. He fought back against the foreign invaders, driving the Vikings out of southern England. Alfred is remembered not only for his military successes, but also for his love of books and his ideas about education. He ruled until his death in 899, and was buried in Wintanceaster, the capital of Wessex. You can see a statue of him in the centre of that city now, and another in Wantage, where he was born.

Some of the towns, villages, and other places in the text are now known by different names:

Wintanceaster is now called Winchester.

Hamwic is called Southampton.

Brycg Stowe, Duibhlinn, and Rone are now called Bristol, Dublin, and Rouen.

The island called Wit is now known as the Isle of Wight. Holeweye and Shamblord are modern Ventnor and Cowes.

West Francia is now part of France, and Carusburc is called Cherbourg.

Ishbiliyah is now called Seville. In 859, Ishbiliyah and Córdoba were both cities in the Muslim-ruled province of Al-Andalus, which is now Andalusia in southern Spain.

ACKNOWLEDGEMENTS

If you want to know more about Alfred the Great, Charles the Bald, Viking swords, Anglo-Saxon bread, or anyone or anything else mentioned in this book, you're in luck. You don't have to travel back in time. You simply have to take a trip to a library, a bookshop, or a museum, or look on the internet, and start searching, exploring, discovering . . .

I read many fascinating books while researching this story, and saw amazing exhibits in museums and galleries, and I'd like to thank all the historians who have uncovered, researched, and illuminated our history.

I'd also like to thank the people who made this book with me. Thank you to everyone at Andersen Press, particularly my editors,

Eloise Wilson and Charlie Sheppard, and Chloe Sackur, who knows much more than me about the Vikings. Thank you, Garry, for your brilliant illustrations. Finally, my thanks and love to Bella, Esther, and Rosie; and a special thank you to our dog Pippi who accompanied me on many long walks while I was dreaming about Thomas, Scarlett, and their adventures.

The Dragonsitter

Josh Lacey

Illustrated by Garry Parsons

Collect them all!

HOPE JONES
SAVES THE WORLD

JOSH LACEY
ILLUSTRATED BY BEATRIZ CASTRO

My name is Hope Jones. I am ten years old. I am going to save the world.

Hope Jones' New Year's resolution is to give up plastic, and she's inspiring others to do the same with her website hopejonessavestheworld.com. When she realises her local supermarket seems to stock more unnecessary plastic than food, she makes it her mission to do something about it. She may be just one ten-year-old with a homemade banner, but with enough determination, maybe Hope Jones really can save the world.

'A lively and heartening read'
Guardian

9781783449279

THE Grk SERIES

JOSH LACEY

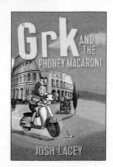

BERLIE DOHERTY
TREASON

Will Montague is a page to Prince Edward, son of King Henry VIII. As the King's favourite, Will gains many enemies in Court. His enemies convince the King that Will's father has committed treason and he is thrown into Newgate Prison. Will flees Hampton Court and goes into hiding in the back streets of London. Lost and in mortal danger, he is rescued by a poor boy, Nick Drew. Together they must brave imprisonment and death as they embark on a great adventure to set Will's father free.

'Doherty paints a very vivid picture . . . almost Shardlake for young readers.'
Independent on Sunday

'A beautifully paced and measured story. 5 stars.'
Books for Keeps